HOOKS AND SLAUGHTERHOUSE

First Montag Press E-Book and Paperback Original Edition January 2013

Copyright © 2013 by Alana I. Capria

As the writer and creator of this story Alana I. Capria asserts the right to be identified as the author of this book.

Montag Press ISBN 978-0-9822809-5-9
Cover design © 2013 Rita Okusako
Author photo © 2013 Alana I. Capria

Montag Press Team:
Project Editor – Alex Paskulin
Illustration & Layout – Rita Okusako
Managing Director – Charlie Franco

A Montag Press Book
www.montagpress.com
Montag Press
536 E. 8th Street
Davis CA, 95616 USA

Montag Press, the burning book with the hatchet cover, the skewed word mark and the portrayal of the long-suffering fireman mascot are trademarks of Montag Press.

Printed & Digitally Originated in the United States of America
10 9 8 7 6 5 4 3 2 1

This book is a work of fiction. Names, characters, places, and incidents are either products of the author's vivid and sometimes disturbing imagination or are used fictitiously without any regards with possible parallel realities. Any resemblance to actual persons, living or dead, events, or locales is entirely coincidental.

HOOKS AND SLAUGHTERHOUSE

ALANA I. CAPRIA

MONTAG

Dedicated to Eddie.

Special thanks to Alex Paskulin for all her work
in making *Hooks and Slaughterhouse* a reality.
And thanks to all the chroniclers of New Jersey
urban legends for keeping the strange alive.

once upon a

hollowed out moon, my liver withers. i touch the meat and it crumbles beneath my fingertips. dust clings to my skin, black fragments chipped and falling. my finger shoves past my lips and enters my throat. bitter powder falls onto my tongue. my tonsils numb. in the dark of my mouth, shadowed by opaque saliva curtains, my finger spreads into a hand, then opens. meat covers everything. i pry the flesh fragments apart. past the meat, propped against a rancid tree foaming around the branches, is a pair of broken owl eyes. glass shards come out of the colored lenses and make a [tinkle] sound when hitting the ground. i wrap old meat around my hips until a skirt drapes across the floor. thin fat pieces, so thin that the individual fibers snap apart and form tiny hollows, resemble lace texture. i place my fingers in the lace and spread my fingers apart, opening the holes. i arrange the skirt around my knees until it is hard to walk. then i do. i walk across a leaf-strewn lawn and my toes ache as the hard ground pushes against them. my breasts burn. i place my hands over my breasts and press against the nipples. sharp pain shoots down my back and into my hips. i pause near a drying oak tree and vomit blood over the base. rancid tar fluid coats the bark and runs to the ground, wetting the dirt until mud puddles suck the roots down. [you are pregnant, the moon whispers] and reaches down to rub the sides of my face. i raise my arms and scratch the moon's face until long blood clot threads rise to the craggy surface. [pregnant with what, i ask.] the moon opens her skeletal mouth and vomits over my head. meaty fluid drains off the moon's tongue. i spit out the red bits that cling to my lips. the moon licks her rocky lips clean and spits the last of the fluid onto the dirt. [with this and that, the moon whispers. dead children. broken tree bits. all those things. the livers and kidneys and kumquat peels. if you breathe deeply enough, you'll smell the pomegranate seeds.] i touch my stomach. i press against my bowels. [but i am infertile, i say.] the moon laughs. she swats several stars away from her face and smacks her teeth together. [too adorable, the moon whispers. yes, infertile. but not your skin. pores have no need for ovaries.] the moon jumps slightly and rocks away, white bulb swaying from left to right until clear. i sit on the floor, festering in the vomit and mud. i cake the mud on my thighs and stack it until it is a tiny mountain of anatomical sludge. my stomach growls. i lean forward and lick the mud off my legs. my vision turns blue, then a faint pinkish red. i curl up in the mud and sink into the earth several feet. [the bloodless girl's burial, a dry voice whispers.] i squeeze my eyes shut. dirt rushes up my nose. i move the dirt away from my mouth and raise my head slightly. [is anyone there, i ask.] my fingers slip in the mud and i fall deeper into the hole. [go back to sleep, the voice says.] i claw the mud sides and pull myself over. i roll onto dry grass. [what did you say, i ask. what did you call me?] several metal flowers slither to my feet. they tap against my ankles until clear fluid drips out of me. the moisture fills the mud puddle hole. i lift one flower. it wilts. [who are you, i ask.] [you are the bloodless girl, a rusted tulip petal says and scrapes.]

how the bloodless
state begins::: first, i cut my wrists in half and black tar pours
out. but it does not pour forever. at the end, it drips and
changes to a deep yellow shade. yellow amber covers the floor.
orange fumes waft away from the fluid and the fumes stink
of fresh orange mixed with raw meat. [everything smells like
meat, i say] but the tree limbs do not acknowledge the obser-
vation. they press against my skin. they tear my wrists into
pieces. chunks drop to the floor. then the yellow is clear and
the more i touch the clear fluid with my fingernails, the harder
it is for me to cover my eyes. the clear fluid is like water. but
it is not like water because it smells like melted candle wax. i
bite my nails. i spit the enamel on the floor. i press my hands
against my thighs and the fluid flows down my skin, soaking
everything, until my flesh is squishy like the meat of a sea
sponge. i bury myself in a rock bed. i stack chunks of granite
around my body, curving the stones until they curve over my
head. the clear fluid fills the space. it pushes through tiny gaps
in the rocks. but the clear fluid dries. the clear fluid dribbles
slowly. each droplet dehydrates until it is a tiny powder granule.
the dust strikes the floor. it covers my chest. i wipe the dust
away and sneeze. powder floats around my self-made cavern. it
covers the walls. i breathe the dust in. i press my hands against
my chest and breathe slowly, forcing the dust in and out of my
lungs until my tongue numbs. a hooked finger pushes through
the rock stones and strokes the sides of my feet. [you should
come out, a voice says.] the finger works up the sides of my
legs, then taps gently against my knees. [come out, the voice
says] and the fingers dig into my flesh. the fingers tug. the
fingers spread into wide hands that grasp my thighs and yank.

the stones roll off the ceiling. they strike the floor and clatter away, rolling downhill while i claw at the hands. [let me go, i cry] and the hands pull my skin harder. my skin tears. i sit up and push the gray stones away from my face. a skeletal pumpkin sits in front of me. it drags its arms back. wormy fingers disappear into its gaping mouth. [hello, the pumpkin says] and leans to one side. it bites the ground with a quick snapping motion, uprooting several poisonous plants and the connecting dirt tendrils. i place my hands over my stomach and press down until my abdomen aches. [what are you, i ask.] the pumpkin rolls its eyes. it looks upward and vomits several times. a slow stream of purple vomit drips from its mouth and soaks into the ground, leaving a scalded purple stain. i place my hand against the stain and the skeletal pumpkin pushes me away. [my vomit, it says] and scoops the sullied dirt up. the dirt drops into its mouth and disappears. a faint red glow covers its pumpkin chest, then dissipates into several elaborate striations. [are you here for the bones, the skeletal pumpkin asks.] i stand up slowly. my feet sink into the ground. [what bones, i ask] yanking my feet up. the skeletal pumpkin rises onto its wooden vines. it slides through the dirt, its stem flexing with effort. [the bones up there, the skeletal pumpkin says] and points straight ahead. i squint and see the outline of a large tree in the middle of a field. [what is it, i ask.] the skeletal pumpkin sighs. [the devil tree. don't tell on me, it says.]

the skeletal pumpkin

pulls me away from the devil tree. i reach for the trunk and the pumpkin knocks my hands away. [you can't touch it, the skeletal pumpkin whispers. that's the kind of tree that bites.] i lean over. a thick fog grows near the edge of the field. slowly, it drifts in our direction, coating the ground with a pale gray cloud. i push the fog away. i stare at the trunk but do not see any teeth tucked into the spaces between the bark. [i don't see anything, i whisper.] the skeletal pumpkin sighs. it roots its body into the ground and disappears into the fog. [you aren't supposed to see the teeth, the skeletal pumpkin whispers, its voice echoing through the field. that's why it is a devil tree.] i reach into the fog and pat the skeletal pumpkin on the head. my hand thumps against its hard enamel and the skeletal pumpkin squeals softly. [can we be friends, it asks.] i lift the pumpkin off the ground and hold it to my chest. the pumpkin vibrates slowly, like a heartbeat, its flesh pulsating until little meat slabs drip out of its carved face. [who carved you, i ask.] [a hand. but it doesn't come from this tree, the skeletal pumpkin whispers. we should go.] the skeletal pumpkin strains to get away from me. i pat its stumpy stem and the skeletal pumpkin sighs. i put it on the ground and the fog covers the gourd again. i turn to the devil tree. the trunk is slightly darker than most trees i have seen in my life. the bark is slightly thicker in some parts but it is not a scary tree. near the back of the tree, a branch extends over the field, the limb pulled down until parallel with the ground. i touch the tree. my hands burn. [is the wood cov-ered with poison, i ask.] the skeletal pumpkin rushes around my feet. it nudges my ankles gently. [we should go, the skeletal pumpkin says.] i push the pumpkin away. i put my hands on the tree and reach up, finding a thick branch to seize. my fingers curl around a bough and i place a foot against the uneven tree surface. [up i go, i say] and pull. the skeletal pumpkin screams. my skin aches. my legs scrape against the tree bark as i climb. my arm entwines around the branch and i drape my chest over the limb. [i'm up, i say.] the skeletal pumpkin leaps out of the fog and moans softly. [but you're going to die now, it says.] i look at my hands. yellowish blisters cover the palms. i tap the burn marks with my nails. the blisters erupt. dust pours out of the holes and covers my hands. [how did i lose so much blood, i ask.] the skeletal pumpkin flips onto its side and whips the fog with its tendrils. [you are dead, the skeletal pumpkin sighs. you've been dead for days. the drying process was the final stage.] i stare at the skeletal pumpkin. i look at my dusty hands. i press my lips together and turn to the tree trunk. my face scrapes against the trunk and i stare into the wood. the wood moves. it rolls beneath my skin. it spreads and in each space, a face stares back at me, mouth stretched until it resembles a salivating crescent moon, the eyes squinted until just tiny squiggles on the face. the faces lunge at me. they bite my lip. tiny fangs, translucent milk-teeth, dig into my lip and gnaw the flesh. i pull back. my skin rips. the faces merge into an eye. the eye blinks several times and its pupil engorges with tree pulp. [you stink of vinegar, the eye says] and pushes me.

i fall onto

the skeletal pumpkin. it pushes me away. we sit in the fog together. condensation covers our faces. [why did you go into the
tree, the skeletal pumpkin asks] and burns its accordion face
with a tiny match plant. i bite the skeletal pumpkin. it presses
its skeletal mouth together and whimpers several times. [i am
not pie, the skeletal pumpkin says. how dare you treat me like
that? do you think i am sugared and baked so that you can have
a culinary delight? i am not. in fact, i am full of parsley. its poison leaves grow out of my seeds. they sprout between my fake
teeth. so i am an abortive thing. you cannot press your tongue
against me without losing your uterus. it's sad. but necessary.
otherwise, everyone would run around trying to peel me open
and eat my contents.] the skeletal pumpkin puts its fingers in
its eyes. i pull its arms apart and pull the pumpkin onto my lap.
[you are so angry, i say] and the skeletal pumpkin sighs. [why
did you go into the tree, it asks.] we look up. the tree glows
with a pale yellow-red light. the light travels from the tree's
base to its branches. the horizontal branch descends slightly,
swinging towards our heads. we duck down. bark faces hiss.
[how dare you touch us, the bark asks. you are pathetic. you
cannot lay a finger on us without having it be bitten off. pathetic. pathetic. we don't even let the virgins get this close.] the
skeletal pumpkin whimpers. its anchovy spine tongue drops
out of its mouth and stabs the fog. [i told you not to climb the
tree. it's such an angry thing. the meat will burn through its
roots and bite you, the skeletal pumpkin says.] it puts its fingers in its eyes and cries softly. i pull its arms out. [would you
stop, i ask. you are being overly dramatic.] the skeletal pumpkin crosses its triangle shapes. its gourd rises and falls several

times. i pat the skeletal pumpkin and stand up. the devil tree hisses. it spits poison plants in my direction. [how dare you try to face us, the bark faces hiss. we never gave you permission to give us a kiss. if anything, we will tear you into pieces and rip your heart out. do not test us. we have a taste for rotten meat.] i touch the devil tree. i place my feet against the trunk and yank myself up. i smack the bark faces. they whimper. their tongues hang out of their mouths and touch the ground. [abuse, the devil tree cries. you are abusing me within an inch of my tree life.] i crawl through the tree branches. i drag my knees over the faces. i climb onto the horizontal branch and hang down, staring at the burned ash floor of the field for several minutes. [is that what you've been trying to protect, i ask.] the devil tree shudders. its leaves move back and forth. paper rustles against the back of my neck. [i like the meat, the devil tree says.] [then what were you trying to get out of me, i ask.] the devil tree rolls over the ground. it bulldozes the fog. the skeletal pumpkin leaps into the air and lands on my back. [you can't eat us, the skeletal pumpkin squeals] and burrows its vines into my waist. i reach over my shoulders and smack the skeletal pumpkin. [stop, i say. you're going to make me bleed.] [no blood, the skeletal pumpkin and tree cry.] they puncture my knees. yellow dust drifts out of my swollen caps. powder slicks over the tree, leaving amber stains. [dust skin, the skeletal pumpkin and the tree say.] i fall down.

the devil tree
lifts its roots out of the ground. it sprinkles my face with dirt. i
wipe the grit away. it catches between my teeth. [i think i would
rather go to the cemetery, i say and the devil tree hisses.] its
bark faces open wide. their cheeks blossom like flowers. [i
knew a red-draped woman once, the devil tree whispers. she
was kind. but she woke me many times in the middle of the
night. no matter how i tossed and turned, she dug her fingers
into my spine.] the devil tree's limbs lower until they brush
over the dirt, tearing the grass up. i pat the tree gently. the
skeletal pumpkin climbs onto my back and plays with the vertebrae pushing out of my spine. [do you think we can have
the bones hiding in your trunk, the skeletal pumpkin asks.] the
devil tree stops. it turns slowly. its bark faces open and close.
[what makes you think i have any bones inside my bark, the
devil tree says.] the skeletal pumpkin ducks down, hiding its
face behind my scapulae. i twist slightly and the skeletal pumpkin falls to the floor. [not nice, the gourd says] and struggles to
pull its weight free of a mud puddle. i grab its stem and yank
the skeletal pumpkin out of the mud. [why do you think i have
bones, the devil tree asks.] the skeletal pumpkin hangs its spinal tongue over the ground. [i assumed, the skeletal pumpkin
says.] it vomits little red clots. i cup my hands together and the
clots rest on my palms. i pat the skeletal pumpkin and it forces
a smile. [do you have any bones, i ask.] the devil tree shakes its
limbs. purple fruits drop off its branches and smash against
the dirt floor. yellow juice pours out of the fruits. it saturates
the ground. orange mud forms. [they are not bones, the devil
tree says. they are bone fruits. there might be bone seeds inside.
but i can't tell. it's a problem for me. my branches don't work

like fingers.] the skeletal pumpkin shuffles forward. it grabs a bone fruit and works its fingers around the peel. it yanks the meat apart and the pith drops to the floor. i lift the pith to my mouth. my lips pucker around the bitter flavor. [it has a strange sweet sour, i say] and swallow. the skeletal pumpkin shatters the fruit. it squeezes the meat and bone seeds pour out. tiny white shapes fill the skeletal pumpkin. they drip onto the floor. i lift one seed and hold it to my eye. the seed has a vague femur shape. i turn the seed around and the moon reaches down to snatch it away. [i have been waiting for a bone seed for eternities, the moon says] and gobbles the bone seed down. the skeletal pumpkin sobs over the seeds. it lifts handfuls to its mouth and drops them onto its lap. [they are bones, the skeletal pumpkin moans. beautiful, juicy, marrow-filled bones. spinal cords and phalanges and clavicles. all in perfect shape.] the skeletal pumpkin drops onto its side and moans. the bones push through the skeletal pumpkin's shell and stick to its tongue. the devil tree watches silently. more fruits roll off the limbs and shatter on the floor. i walk to the tree. i wrap my arms around it and stroke the tree bark until it flakes. [i will miss the bone meat, the devil tree says] and shudders. i sit on the roots. i place my head against the trunk. [the skeletal pumpkin is very happy, i say.] the devil tree nods. [i was not always bloodless, i say. i must look for a red place to become whole again.] the devil tree does not move. [do you know one, i ask.] a pomegranate rolls into my lap.

i skewer the

pomegranate seeds on a long devil tree stem. black rods stick out of the bulbous red flesh. fresh juice pours out of the entry points. the skeletal pumpkin gnashes its meaty teeth. [i have never seen anything so bloody before, the skeletal pumpkin whispers] and sticks a flower into its back to bleed. orange blood pours out of the hole. i toss the pomegranate seeds over my shoulder. the devil tree sighs. [that is not right, the devil tree whispers. you just sacrificed the pomegranate seeds to the winding road. not right. the shadows, they are so hungry past that corner. and they will maul the seeds until there is barely a droplet of juice left.] the devil tree crosses its bark with its horizontal plank. its branches scrape over its trunk and wood chips drop onto my head. [how did you become the bloodless girl, the devil tree asks] and turns away from the shadowed road. i stand up. i wipe pomegranate juice off my hands. [such a waste, the skeletal pumpkin whispers. and my tongue is terribly blistered with these messy products.] the skeletal pumpkin drops onto its left side and rubs its meaty cheeks against the floor for several hours. i watch the pumpkin pulp drain out of the skeletal head. [your teeth will fall out if you aren't careful, i say] and the skeletal pumpkin lifts its head. i step over its vegetative body and slide my feet through several thick mud puddles. [where are you going, the skeletal pumpkin asks] and stands up. it swallows its vines and vomits old bone fruits. the devil tree spins in circles. [where are you going, it asks] and shakes its branches in my direction. i step over its roots. [i'm going to walk up that road, i say. it may lead to a slaughterhouse.] the skeletal pumpkin gasps. its spinal tongue drops onto the dirt. [you cannot go there, the skeletal pumpkin breathes.] [there are bulbous children around the dark corners, the devil tree says. they are hideous things with huge round eyes and black spots over their mouths. when they talk, it is like crunching teeth.] the devil tree falls over. it lands on the skeletal pumpkin. they lie in the dirt, clutching at one another with their roots and vines. i dig in the dirt beneath their bodies and tear several orange flowers up. [our botanical children, the skeletal pumpkin and tree whine. it isn't fair. you bite everything.] they slump down. their heads strike the ground and shatter into many pieces. i place the orange petals on my tongue. they melt into my mouth meat and leave a thick fatty residue across the flesh. i run my nails over the surface and pick the meat apart. the skin tears. my lips ache. [the shadow road calls, i say.] the skeletal pumpkin bleats like a sheep. it smacks its skull against the ground until a tiny section splinters in a spiderweb pattern. [i'll come back, i say.] i tear a yellow leaf off the devil tree and tuck it into my back. the skeletal pumpkin plays with an assortment of rounded dirt clots. [do you promise, the skeletal pumpkin asks.] it opens its mouth and i look past its burned-down candle sticks to the small mound of blackened wicks covering its fibrous sinew and innards. [i promise, i say. the road isn't that far away. i'll walk from one end to the other and if i don't find my blood, i'll turn back.] the devil tree sobs. its droplets drown the skeletal pumpkin. i walk to the shadow at edge of the field and step onto the heartbeat road. dusty organs crunch.

hear the rhythmic
tapping of the concrete heartbeats. hmm, hmm, hmm, thud.
hmm, hmm, hmm, thud. all beneath the streets, tucked deep
within the heartbeat road while the pious children hang their
heads in shame while hooking pulmonary stones onto their
thin muscled tongues. [ring around the rosy, we baked ashes
into posies, corpses, corpses, the bones fall down, the children whisper] and slap raw meat onto the tops of their heads.
[where did the hearts go, i ask.] the children point at their bulbous stomachs. i step around their skeletons and the children
sit on the ground. they play with their hair, pulling the strands
out of their scalps and placing them gently on the ground. [it
is a voodoo street, the children whisper] and wrap their hair
strands around a small rock by their feet. i walk slowly. the road
stretches for thousands of feet and a thin fog hovers above
the concrete. despite the condensed air, i can still see how dark
the ground is. the road curves to the right and i follow a tiny
line of grass marking the road's outer boundary. at the curve,
which turns at a sudden right angle, i sit on the ground and cry.
a tiny moon rock gnaws at my stomach pit and the piercing
pain moves into my chest until it feels as though my lungs are
swollen with water. i gag and the children look up. [what is that,
they ask one another. the water? is that normal? what is the
fluid called?] the children push their nails into their eye sockets and move the digits around for several moments, scram-
bling the gelatin until light white fluid pours down their cheeks.
[does our pain make you feel better, the children ask.] i rub my
eyes with my fist and the gravel stuck to my skin gets into my
eyelids. my eye burns and squeezes shut. i pull my eyelids apart,
forcing the skin away from the lashes, and dry gravel rolls out.

it strikes the floor and slides away. the children play with their thigh bones. i sniffle. the children run down the road. they grab my arms and pull me off the ground. [it was cold anyway, i say] and pat my backside several times until my fingers are just as cold. i wipe my eyes again and salt crystals flake off my skin. i scratch my neck and round the corner. the children follow, their hands touching my ankles as i walk. i smile at the children and they blow air out of their eyes. [do you think we can come with you to the other side, the children ask] and twist their tongues into a pretzel shape. i look behind and the fog thickens. it rises into the air, creating a draped wall that separates the concrete from the trees, the shadowy branches from the sky. [i don't think you have a choice, i say. the way back is blocked.] the children peek over their shoulders and spit red fluid onto the ground. [how disgusting, the children say. we told that fog to go away. it is too angry for our tongues to swallow.] the children stoop over and gather several handfuls of rocks. they shove the stones onto their tongues. their cheeks bulge. [you eat the fog, i ask. what does it taste like?] the children hiss. [we never said we eat anything, the children say.] they bite my wrists and my skin spreads apart like paper. i pull the dry pieces and drop them. they drift to the floor. the road beats. my feet pulse. the children hold hands. they cross their eyes and at the end of the bend, we face a wooden bridge.

with children clinging
to my ankles, i crawl across the wooden bridge. planks sag beneath my feet. wooden edges buckle and drop slightly, nearing the waterline. i hold my breath and cling to the skewered railings. at the bridge center, the children flop onto the unsteady floor and hold their hands over their mouths. [do you smell it, they mumble.] a dull ache catches my abdomen. i clench my hands together and press them to my waist. [it is a cyst, i whisper] and lean forward slightly to relieve the torso pressure. the children roll their eyes. [a cyst, they ask. it isn't a cyst. it is a rotten meat stench. tell us you can't smell it.] and i cannot smell it. i stretch my neck and lift my chin but the smell does not become stronger. [i can't smell anything, i say] and the children smack their chins against the wood until the skin breaks. i pull the children by their head hair. they leap to their feet and shake their shoulders. [you'll break the floor that way, i say] and the children force smiles. [we want to swim, the children say.] i point at the water. [then jump over, i say.] i step away from the railing. the children press against the barrier and peer over. dark water churns against the bridge legs, foaming at the surface, then dropping into wells and small falls. the children's lips press flat. they shake their heads. [no. we do not trust black water. especially not at night. we won't be able to tell the surface from the dirt bottom. we might as well swim in a black hole. then we'll have to swim forever and maybe we will pass you but maybe we won't and by then exhaustion will bloat our skin, the children say.] bridge planks shake as we walk. i keep my hand to my aching uterus. [this cyst grows larger by the second, i say.] the children pluck marrow out of their noses and fling the yellow fat onto the ground. [we don't know what

cysts are. because we are children. and have never had anything to do with our anatomical nature before, the children say. it is sad. but we come to terms with our shortcomings. we know bone and skin. that is all. and meat. what more is there to concern ourselves with?] the children's tongues slap around their mouths until their skin bruises with deep red marks. [red mark, red mark, do you have some skin? no bruise, no bruise, you still win. i went to a market, then asked for an ax. the man gave me sausage, i gave him a whack. red mark, red mark, have you any skin? no bruise, no bruise, the blood is dim, the children recite.] they pull their hair until their scalp skin stretches. i smack their hands. the children sob. tears flow down their faces. they stick their fingers into their cheeks and drag their muscle down until their jaws have tripled in size. [you are mean, the children say. and we do not like the way you look at us when we think of steaks.] the children fling themselves onto the ground. their spines undulate up and down, breaking the bridge wood until the children are faced with the tiny sinusoid pieces in the wood grain. [our meat, they ask.] they stick their fingers into their mouths and chew. the wood cracks. it pulses and flings me onto the shore. the children wrap their limbs around the wood pulp. [goodbye, the children shout. we are going downstream.] the children drop into the water. i turn to the hilltop. a silver building stares at me. its rusted factory doorways open slowly. i walk.

sometimes i forget
about the skeletal pumpkin. those are the days where i am
surrounded by hungry radiators and glass windows refuse to
break. then i think of the skeletal pumpkin and his glowing orange parts hum in the dark. [do you think about me, the skeletal
pumpkin asks] and its voice echoes in the dark, bouncing off
metal slabs, then collapsing against the ceilings. i scratch my
wrists and the skeletal pumpkin fades away. i sit on the floor. i
crawl beneath a flight of skeletal metal steps and sit on a dust
mound. through several long cracks in the walls, i watch the
sun rise and fall. pink light covers the stone by my face, then
fades into a purple-gray, before turning black. i bat the colors
away. i rest my head on the back of the step and roll my eyes
several times. [you were supposed to return from the bridge,
the skeletal pumpkin says] and the floor opens slightly. i slide
away from the opening. my feet drop through and a cold draft
moves up my legs, chilling my skin. [you aren't supposed to be
here, i say. i left you at the field.] the skeletal pumpkin sighs.
its orange tendrils extend out of the hole and wrap around my
ankles. [it's time to come back, the skeletal pumpkin whispers]
and pulls. i sever the pumpkin vines with my nails. the tendrils
drop through. the floor seals with a loud concrete snap. i cling
to the stairs. i climb up the back way and soon my head scrapes
against the basement ceiling. before i was a bloodless girl and
long before the skeletal pumpkin, i was just a uterus with arms
and legs. i walked long dirt roads without looking at anything
but my ankles. the bones grated together. bone shards covered
the ground. my tongue was infertile then. i chewed but could
not swallow. i clasped the muscle to my chest and prodded the
meat until a water droplet rolled off but even then, the meat

wasn't moist. so i put my tongue away. i tucked it beneath a bed
of rusted silver nails and forgot i ever had any skin at all. so
my flesh felt better and my wrists were lighter and now, when
i think of wombs, i think of steak, not my lack of femininity.
i move through the stairs and slide across the nearest floor.
my chest rubs against the tiles. [why didn't you bring us with
you, the skeletal pumpkin asks.] its gourd splinters and orange
shell scatters across the tiles. i grab the pieces and tuck them
beneath my chin. the skeletal pumpkin moans. it flops on the
floor and it falls apart in the field. [i'm trying to keep you alive,
i say. you were the one who didn't want to be baked into a pie.]
the skeletal pumpkin sobs. it wipes its eyes. i look away from
the windows and the thin canvas sheets covering the spaces.
[we imagined you being healthier, the walls say] and bricks fall.
i kick the bricks away from my skin. they collapse into dust
clots. [is this in mockery, i ask.] the walls shake the factory. [of
course not, they whisper. we wouldn't dream of teasing you.]
the dust clots gather powder. residue clings to the tiny center and grows in size. my head moves in circles. i stare at the
stairs and they drift off to the left, then shift to the right. [are
the stairs deformed, i ask.] [you are, the walls whisper.] they
whip the air with the staircase railing. the air bleeds. [everything
mocks me. even the inanimate has fluid, i say.] i bite the stairs
and run away.

walls close in

around me. i turn and silver covers me. i duck down and gold falls onto my shoulders. bronze smears my face. then rust falls. the rust falls like snow, drifting down and dusting the stairs with a faint brown hue. i brush the rust off my face and the flecks taint my hands. [i have grown the metallic shimmer, i whisper] and tilt my head upward. i stare at the ceiling. the tiles sag. concrete pillars drop down from the next floor and fall close to my head. i touch the pillars and they pierce my hands. dust clots rise up from my palms. i flick the dust away. metallic voices fill the room. [why isn't she asleep, the voices ask. shouldn't she be asleep? as soon as she gets pricked, out like a light. prick her again! use the floorboards. she has a ceiling immunity. or... or not. use a meat hook. that would work. just stick her hand. no, not her hand. her finger. it has to be her finger or else she might stay awake. maybe. she can stay awake forever if we aren't careful. but she has to go to sleep.] i turn around and narrowed pink eyes move around the shadows, stepping in and out of the windows, passing by the doorways. [i can see you, i say.] the eyes stop moving. they blink and disappear. [now can you see us, the voices ask.] [your eyes are closed. so no, i say.] the voices sigh. the eyes reappear. i see the faintest hint of eyelid spreading apart to reveal the pink color. [are you tired, the voices ask. you look sleepy.] i fling my arm out and catch an eye with my fingertip. the eye squeezes shut and a voice moans loudly. [not fair, the voices say. you bit.] i wipe my finger on my thigh. [i didn't bite. i poked, i say.] the voices sigh. the eyes scrape over the floor. [are you singular gelatin orbs or are there other limbs i cannot see, i ask.] i sit on the floor. metal dust pushes through my skin and pokes my inner muscles. i imagine tiny threads wrenching their way through my vein and wriggling upward until i vomit from the pain. i shift my hips and the metal falls out. i sweep it away. the eyes gather around me. they press close. they blink rapidly and their shadowed lids fan my skin. [we are just orbs, the eyes say. and we are sad about it. we want to be more than orbs.] the eyes flutter. they soar around the room, bumping into metal hooks and breaking glass panes. [be better, the eyes scream. orbs. better orbs. better us. us orbs. orbs us. orbs better. ah!] they fall to the concrete and roll for several feet until their gelatin pushes against me. i poke the eyes. i poke each pink mound once and clean my finger on the floor. [why wipe, the orbs ask. we aren't dirty.] i hold my finger in the air. [you are wet, i say. and moisture doesn't suit me.] the pink orbs spread apart. they press against the concrete walls and scale the textured molding until they dangle from the ceiling edges. [why doesn't it suit you, the orbs ask.] i link my fingers and crack them individually. dust grates in the bones. it makes a soft shhhhh sound as it slides back and forth in the hollow. [because i have dust inside, i say.] the pink eyes turn to one another. [the bath, they ask. yes, yes. the bath! of course. the blood? not the blood. the water. liquid in general. the bath! here, metal!] the pink orbs rush to my shoulders. [we know a blood tin, they whisper. you can bathe in it.] they point to the stairs.

pink eye orbs

bring me to the basement stairs. [i was down there before, i say] turning away from the steps. the pink eye orbs shake. [no, no, they whisper. you weren't down there. it was another down there. something tucked away in the intestines. a place you shouldn't have gone. but this place, we are telling you it is okay. because we want you to go.] they push me onto the first step. i back onto the landing. [i don't want to go down there, i say. i know i was down there. i remember those stairs. the third step was discolored by a red paint stain.] the pink eye orbs gesture. [then go look, they say. we want to see the red paint.] they glide down the stairs. i move my black hair behind my shoulders and step down. the pink orbs hum. their vibrations travel up the stairs and shake me as i walk. i cling to the thin skeletal railing. [this is the same metal spine i held onto before, i say.] the pink eye orbs drop to the basement bottom and rest on the floor. i count the stairs. [three, six, seventeen, i whisper.] at step number thirty-nine, i am three steps away from the bottom. i step down but there is no red paint. i turn slightly and look at the step above me. a blue paint smear covers the metal. [maybe the paint was blue instead of red, i say.] the pink eye orbs hum. they brush over the walls. [liar, they sing. there was never any paint at all. you're making that all up.] i stare at the paint. i press my fingertips against it and the paint smears. i put the smear on my legs. the blue fades into a clear white color. then the white darkens to a pale foggy gray. [you painted it, i say.] the pink eye orbs shake from left to right. [no, they whisper. we didn't do anything of the kind. we are only orbs. we do not grow paint. can you grow paint? can you pull it out of your eyes? is that possible? we don't know. but the thought makes us cry.] the pink eye orbs flutter. they glide up and down the railing, slicking the metal with pink solvent. the acid burns through the metal. rust sizzles. i place my hands in the fluid but it feels like water. i flick the fluid in the air. the pink eye orbs dart away. [are you trying to kill us, they ask.] the fluid touches the ceiling and fizzles. [she was trying to kill us, the pink eye orbs say. she thought she could use our fluids to burn us. that is not right. that is not nice.] the pink eye orbs drop to the ground. they flounder in a thick dust bath, their eyes stretching with fluid retention, then draining until squished. i scoop the pink eye orbs up and drop them onto my shoulders. they burrow into my epidermis, moving the skin until it forms a slight cone shape. [you are warm, the pink eye orbs say. we like that. you are very warm. like a fleshy blanket. one we can make friends with.] the pink eye orbs hug my ligaments. i pat their heads gently. [can we take you to the meat lands, the pink eye orbs ask.] i look at the broken ceiling. large patches of dark space fill the center of the tiles. the fallen pieces litter the floor. i move the tiles aside and shove my hand into the center. the tiles shift. their laminate bodies, thick with dust clusters, slide across the ground. dust falls off the tiles. particles fill the air. my chest aches and i breathe deeply. my nose itches. i scratch the bridge and sneeze. [and the girl gives birth to the yellow orbs, the pink eye orbs shout proudly.]

little men wearing

top hats and no clothing run around my ankles. they pull their bodies out of the walls and shiver several times before rubbing their spines over the granite bedding. they jump onto my foot and hop down, their eyes rolling wildly. the little men dig their fists into the concrete and roll stone scrapings into a ball. [what are those, i ask.] the pink eye orbs gesture at the opposite wall. [the homunculi, they say] and light matches with their eyelid tongues. i pat the little men on their heads. they wrench their jaws open and snap them shut on my hand. [we did not warn you, the pink eye orbs say. they bite. the homunculi always bite. fertile little things. with a bad appetite. they want to eat everything. even rocks. especially rocks. hard things are good for their teeth.] i shake the homunculi off my wrists. [but i am not a hard thing, i say.] the pink eye orbs giggle. [who said the homunculi discriminate against textures, the pink eye orbs say. we told you they'll eat anything. bottomless pits, those little monsters. but we like them. they try to tear our lashes out and braid them into necklaces other pupils can wear.] the pink eye orbs tear. clear fluid pours out of the skin and floods the floor. i jump onto the stairs. the homunculi raise their arms and drift with the fluid. [we drown, they scream. we drown. no air. that lack. air follicles. such pain.] the homunculi drop their eyes into the fluid and duck beneath the surface. their backsides float. [flotation device, the homunculi bubble.] their voices burst from the water and splash against the walls. orange droplets drip down. i cover my eyes. [water comes. but how. hungry man. stomach limp. that said. we sleep, the homunculi say.] they flip onto their backs and stare at the ceiling. their eyes bloat. pink eye orbs rush up my arms. they pick at my pores and open the sweat holes. their tongues riddle my flesh. i grab their tongues with my fingernails and yank until the muscle rips in half. the homunculi paddle to the steps. they grab onto the lower step with their teeth and haul themselves down. i bring my foot onto the top of their heads and push them into the water. [we drown. she push. not right. too much. water slosh. lung pressure. the air. it dies, the homunculi say.] they dive to the floor and pull rocks over their waists. their eyes bulge. the gelatin flows to the surface and foams. the pink eye orbs drain off my fingertips. they skim the surface with their lower lashes and the gelatin collects on the hair. the pink eye orbs drop the gelatin onto my hands. i smear the clumps over the walls. [how do i get across, i ask.] i point at a tiny doorway bobbing above the surface. the pink eye orbs rub themselves over the walls un-til dry. they hook their eyelashes into my clothing and lift up. i hang beneath the pink eye orbs. [we will fly you there, the pink eye orbs say] and vibrate across the ceiling. my clothing tugs. i glance down and the water churns beneath me. it splashes me. i bring my legs up and tuck my knees against my chest. i scratch the cartilage. fat drips down. [are you going to come with me, i ask.] the pink eye orbs hover in the concrete doorway frame. [we shouldn't leave the homunculi alone, the pink eye orbs say. but they're so needy. and bite. we will come. we tire of the hooks in the walls.] they fling me through.

to the dead

things i lost before i became bloodless: i see a window made of broken glass within the doorway and the longer i stand by this glass, the longer the internal teeth become until little pieces of flesh hack my limbs open. i keep a knife in my back pocket but it is only because i like to stab fallen fruits and put them out of their rotten misery. no fruit should die before it is cut into segments and peeled. but let the seeds suffer. because they root in lungs and wind around the internal organs without worrying that a monster might grow from the buds. sometimes, a monster comes out of me. it is bright red. it has carmine undertones. bits of orange strewn around. and a face. there is always a face. mine. yours. even little gray things i haven't named yet. the spaetzle pieces. the pretzel nubs. and the skin flesh. but not the skin flesh. the bone monster. the mustard face. and i sit on the floor, sobbing until my eyes fall out. i feed those to the skeletal pumpkin and it thumps its vines in approval while i wrap black thread around my tongue until the blood flow restricts. then it is goodbye. everything, even my knees, which i am partial to. i go to the devil tree and it brings my flesh to its branches, then sheds thirteen layers of dry bark until the skin tosses its pigmentation onto the dirt floor. i tell rocks i miss them. i tell rocks i remember them. then i go to the radiators and tell them the same. radiators do not like affection. if you try to kiss them, radiators will hum until you burn. then you have nothing but a radiator mark and no metal. everything has to have metal. it has to be pulled into a palm or buried in the backyard. but it has to be metal and if it is not metal, it should be skin, and even then, there is no purpose. no metal, no skin. no skin, no metal. and no bastard faces rising out of lamp posts in some pastoral scene heavy with blood clots and broken bones. i used to be heavy with blood clots. but they dried into uterine stones my body refused to pass. so my cervix constricted and my genitals stitched shut. no more entry point. no way to get from the living to the dead, from the bedroom to that space beyond the grave. because they were not important. because they had no nails to share after the rust faded like melting wax. thus. thus. i miss you. hair, skin, stomach and all. wooden parts. red eyes. the entire length of bare ribs. until the muscle is naked and i have nothing left but a sewerage drain tucked into my right ankle, which is swollen with retained dust and remorse. sometimes, i sit on a stone floor and cry until powder comes out of my face. when i do that, my skin tears and the ripped meat dribbles out. i throw it into a frying pan. i scald it with hot oil and boiling water. then i toss the meat at the walls. it sticks like wallpaper. [give me a slaughterhouse, the meat says] and so i listen. that is where i send you. in a cardboard box marked in blood stains so faint they resemble a lemon yellow-gray. i cannot help that. i push what i have to into the fire and tuck black crepe into my eyes to catch the granules. [i am sick, i say.] the mirrors know remorse and they know steak grades. the mirrors stab gray flesh with their frames and i pull my hair until a handful of strands falls onto the glass. [in case you need another me, i say.] and the mirror leaps into the fire.

the space beyond

the doorway churns. yellow light spills out. the pink eye orbs
cluster behind me. [it smells wrong in here, they say] and flutter.
i yank their eyelashes out. the pink eye orbs moan. [not nice,
they say. you are not being nice. we left the slaughter hooks for
you. we left the little men. be nice.] they push my elbows. i look
at the floor. bleached white tiles spread out in thirteen different directions marked by a silver stone door. [it is too bright in
here, the pink eye orbs complain. our eyes hurt. we cannot face
the light. we are not prepared for this kind of visual abuse. can
we turn back?] i lift my hair away from my neck and the pink
eye orbs rush to fill the space. they cluster against my skin, their
lashes pricking the back of my head until dust runs down my
flesh. [you can't pierce me, i say] and the pink eye orbs fasten
their lashes tightly. my hair falls around them. i walk and my
feet echo on the ground. the tiles shimmer. golden light glows
between the individual tiles. [tiny suns. stuck in the ground, the
pink eye orbs whisper into my dead sweat glands.] i spit and a
dirt clot strikes the floor. it leaves a gray stain where the white
should be. [pick a number from one to thirteen, i say.] the pink
eye orbs pulsate. [pumpkin, they say. thirteen! but what about a
tree? three! no, it should be the fourth floor. you do not get to
pick six.] my head aches. i press my hands against my hair, si-
lencing the pink eye orbs. they push against my skin, mumbling
softly. [i'll pick, i say. let's follow the number eight.] i count
from left to right, from right to left, then start again from the
beginning, working my way clockwise. i choose a doorway three
steps away from where i entered. [hold on, i say] and the pink
eye orbs wind their lashes into my hair before biting my back
neck flesh. i walk up the path and the tiles seem to grow as i

move. [do not go any farther, the pink eye orbs scream.] i stop. [why, i ask.] the pink eye orbs jump away from my hair. [this is the cemetery road, they say. we can smell it. there is too much dirt through there. you won't like it. it is very dry. everything in there. turn back. choose another road. anything but that one.] the pink eye orbs seep thick tears. they move in circles, their irises rolling in a vortex-like manner. [i already chose. this is the path we're taking, i say.] the pink eye orbs moan and drop onto the floor. they spread their skin over the tiles. [it absorbs us, they say and the tiles swell with fluid.] i lift the pink eye orbs up. [you're all so precious, i say. but the floor isn't eating you.] i touch the shimmering door and push it open. the doorway splits into thirds, then falls flat. i step onto the walkway. the tiles change into dirt. i kick the dirt and it fills the air, whirling around me before drifting back onto the floor. the walls stop. a pinkish horizon grows out of the broken concrete. dark grave silhouettes push out from the horizon. my eyes follow a purple streak across the top of sky. the pink eye orbs fall to the dirt. they languish on the ground, their pupils swelling and shrink- ing while salt crystallizes on their lashes. [we are going to die, they say.] i glance over the many gravestones. in the center of the cemetery, propped up slightly, a cave-like tomb ruptures from the earth. [the dead nun, the pink eye orbs whimper.] the dead nun lifts her arms.

conversation with a

dead nun crawling out of her tomb in the middle of the harvest moon, her bowels hanging off her hands, blood-slicked
glass tucked into her mouth::: BLOODLESS GIRL: did you
sacrifice meat to the intestinal moon tonight? DEAD NUN:
a demon with a child's face flies tonight. his wings scratch my
face. i gave him my uterus as a coal oven but his meat refused
to cook properly. everything stayed raw. even my cysts. so i released my religious collar and the glass radiator fractured into
several coffins filled with ash. tree ash. not the dead man's.
and even then the stepmother, nailed to the bedroom floor
with a rusted ax, her face screwed on backwards, begged for
a piece of rusted metal to flay her forehead into steak cuts.
BLOODLESS GIRL: i cried. i cried in front of the children
and they wished for a vinegar splash poured straight from my
stomach. i thought of all the dead flesh i had known through-
out my life and if i let that dead skin cling to me for too long,
i might not be able to pour my muscles out of my mouth.
do you know if the crypt can fit me after i leave the skeletal pumpkin in his bloody patch? DEAD NUN, tearing her
knees apart: i think i know you. you are the girl pulled apart
and thrown over the bridge face. BLOODLESS GIRL: i have
nothing to do with bridges. that is some other womb, maybe
a pair of fallopian tubes more fertile than i could ever stretch
over. DEAD NUN, piercing her eyes with a pair of glass ro-
sary beads: a womb? who said anything about a womb? that is
the skin no one should ever try to command in the middle of
the night. after all, what monster grows out of the bed boards?
the goat devil. if you had seen its eyes when it wiped the am-
niotic fluid off its face, you would understand. it hissed and its

loins bit, then its stomach snapped. there was no more mother, just some ribs tucked into the plaster wall and left to fester in a condensed marrow puddle. BLOODLESS GIRL: what if i were to become her? i can make a goat devil come out of me. i have enough candles tucked beneath my tongue. i named the devil tree after my genitals. and if i stare at the ceiling for too long, then i can create a hungry slaughterhouse out of the sagging tiles. that is where you will find all my meat. now let me defecate until my stomach groans with the constant effort. DEAD NUN, winding around the dead girl, playing with her face: are you sure i have never been in your uterus before? because if i can dig my fingers into the meat, then i might be able to pray to your kidney gods. BLOODLESS GIRL: let me defecate in peace. DEAD NUN, her hands filled with rotten shit: defecate? what were you doing before? BLOODLESS GIRL: how do i get to the aluminum slaughterhouse in the distance? DEAD NUN, licking her palms: the one with blood or without? BLOODLESS GIRL: whichever might have a piece of dried and salted skin hanging from the walls. DEAD NUN: do you plan on eating the meat? BLOODLESS GIRL: no. i only want to stare at it until i can see into the next world. DEAD NUN: then reach between your liver and spleen. it is somewhere past that hill. resist cutting your hands on the spiked walls.

long before i

was the bloodless girl, i was a bloody girl. saliva filled my eyes
and vomit spilled out of my nose. i evacuated my uterus thirteen times a day because the cervix was prone to overflowing
with loose tissue and vaginal juice. the procedure was painful.
i ate too many poisonous parsley flakes, then licked a radiator
in the hope that rust would force the blood. and soon, i was
bleeding. i used to bleed into a tub. it was four times larger than
i could ever hope to be and as long as i held onto the sides, the
blood slipped out easily. if i raised an arm or moved a leg, then
clots would fill my stomach until it felt as though kidney stones
were trying to pass. because i was filled with so much fluid, i
was always sick and fluid-heavy cysts covered my inner organs.
they ruptured more times than i could count on one hand so i
wadded up canvas towels and put them deep inside my abdomen. i used to think that if i added fabric, the cysts might dry,
but instead fluid saturated the towels and became a new fluid
tumor that i had to pop with a needle to get out. so the towels
that went in white and blue, or black and yellow, or even green
and pink, came out soaked with red. i strung them up on my
bedroom walls as a reminder of my situation. then i sat with
my legs in the air and pushed until it felt like my uterus would
drop out of my abdominal cavity. but it never did. it stayed
put, rooted in position, and the longer i pushed, the more my
spine filled with clear fluid that helped the vertebrae to run up
and down the whip, milking the column until the fluid dripped
off my tongue. i will say it now. that fluid numbed everything
it touched. it was the world's first organic anesthetic. and i collected it in cups, then drank. maybe i could have twisted to one
side and drained the spine right onto my tongue but i wasn't

ready for the commitment, not when i had pipes that had suddenly refused to work and i couldn't get a bowel movement out sans a wide-necked shovel. i had a mother, too. but she was a limp yellow worm who squirmed on the kitchen windowsill while vomiting. sometimes she reared into the air and her center split in two to allow a new body out of the tube. none of my siblings looked like me. there were five thousand of them, and each had skin that was not skin, and legs that were not legs, and faces that were not faces but nun hoods worn low over their necks. each one had a sucker mouth. the siblings would latch onto my arms as if i were a cow. then they would drink. they tried draining me but i had so much fluid that they drowned instead of fed. then fluid spurted out of their skin and i pricked them with needles before holding them over a sink drain. [you should be nice, the mother worm sighed.] she tried reaching up to touch my face but i did not like physical affection and sprinkled salt around the room so that she had no choice but to stay on a single slab, wriggling her worm tail until the lax muscle cramped. she got tired. of the persistently spawning children, of the windowsill, of me. then i went bloodless. i stood over the oven for too long and everything dried to a thick crust. the mother worm stabbed her heart but did not die. one day while sobbing, she heaved herself over the ledge and dried. her corpse resembled a salt crystal.

i sit on

the dead nun's lap. her moldy skin falls onto my face. i bat the
green flesh away. [you remind me of my old mother worm, i
say. she was a good worm. my birth was quick. but she got sick.
and died. i poured salt over her. i wanted to salt her until she
was preserved. it didn't work.] i press my head against the dead
nun's neck. she pats my face gently. her fingers fall apart by my
mouth. i spit the dead digits away. [have you been rotting for
a long time, i ask.] the dead nun sighs. her dried lungs heave.
they crush into powder. she wheezes and dust flies out of her
nostrils. [you don't know your uterus, the dead nun says.] the
pink eye orbs stay tucked behind the other graves, watching
through holes in the stone. their lashes fan the ground. grass
spins towards me. i close my eyes. the dead nun sticks her fingers against my face and forces my lids apart. [do you know
the uterus, she asks.] i shake my head. [it's defective. the skin
is dried. it doesn't know fluid, i say.] the dead nun grinds her
teeth together. enamel dust coats her lips. the dead nun hums
in her rib cage. the vibrations cross her flesh and burn my
wrists. i hold the stained skin to my mouth and lick until the
tongue's abrasive flesh tears the blisters in half. the dead nun
forces her jaws open. her bones squeak as they move. she lifts
her tongue and the meat sounds like rusted metal rubbing over
a wire fence. dehydrated hearts drop out of her throat. they
thump upon hitting the floor. dirt settles around the organs.
i poke the skin and the jerky-like surface pushes back. [where
did the hearts come from, i ask.] the dead nun pinches her eyes.
gelatin dribbles out of the sockets. [are you looking for a way
through the badlands, she asks.] i look over her shoulder. the
graveyard stretches for thousands of miles. tombstones stand

like trees, concrete bulk dark against the pinkish sky, inscriptions faded. the dirt stays brown. there is no green. [what will i find in the badlands, i ask.] the dead nun sighs. she plays with the little hearts on the ground. one drags its way over to me and thumps against my skin until i lift it. i hold the heart carefully, not squeezing, just supporting it while it stands in midair. [eat me, the heart says.] red blood flows out of its chambers and over my hands. i shake my hand dry, knocking the heart away. the dead nun stares. [those are my organ pieces, she says. you should eat them. they'll be insulted if you don't.] the heart lies on its side, pumping fluid into the dirt. thick mud swirls. i put my fingers in my mouth and suck the salt off the skin. i barely scrape the crystals. my fingers ache and the skin peels back. [i can't eat that, i say. it has too much fluid. and i'm dry. i can't ingest anything with liquid.] the dead nun tears her arm at the socket. she heaves the arm over her head and the flesh smacks the heart's center. the heart wriggles its way into the open hand. [eat me, it says] and the fingers spear the heart's ventricles, pulling it apart. meat falls onto the ground. [you'll find all the things you want in the badlands, the dead nun says. but you can't get there without cutting your eyes first.] the dead nun shakes her limbs. the heart crumbles into dust. her arm crawls towards me, palm open to show the dust mound. i lean forward and inhale. my stomach aches. in the dead nun's bones, the devil tree waves at me.

the dead nun

opens her bones to me. i climb inside and close my eyes. i fall
asleep. it is a quick sleep. it is a drifting sleep and the devil tree
appears in the foggy bloom, limbs spread wide to cover the
dead nun's internal sky. the devil tree tries to understand :::
[what are you looking for, the devil tree asks] picking bones out
of its bark and tossing the calcium onto the ground. i pick the
skin around my nails. i rock back and forth as dust dribbles out
of the wounds. [something made of metal, i say] and bite my
thumb around the nail. the devil tree shakes. [no. but why, the
devil tree asks. what does it mean to your bones?] its bone fruits
ripen around their edges and soft peels drip onto the floor. my
heart beats wildly. i watch fluid drip out of the meat. i want that.
the fluid. the fruits are more watery than i can ever be. the devil
tree picks my skin with its wooden roots. little spikes tear my
muscle into pieces. the slashes stay dry. [if i can find the aluminum vats filled with blood in the slaughter place's bowels, then
i can hydrate myself and stop being the bloodless girl, i say.] the
devil tree presses its limbs together. it breathes slowly and noxious fumes come off the fruits. [why would you want to stop
being the bloodless girl? that is why we like you, the devil tree
says.] it pinches my skin and gray dust flows out of the broken
flesh. [that is what we like. the dust, the devil tree says, clapping
its limbs. because you are lovely when dust covered. and we only
know you as a powdered substance. do not look for the blood.
it will only make your skin pucker. if anything pushes into your
skin, the blood will come out. it's easier to drain blood than
dust.] i sit on the floor. i play with a metal piece stolen from the
hilltop factory. i twirl the piece between my fingers. i move it
back and forth, humming loudly, and when a sharp edge cuts

me, i twist my fingers upward and snap them off. gray dust covers my hands. it clings to my skin. i shake my arms and the dust bursts into the air like mold spores. dust covers the devil tree. [mate with my bark, the devil tree whispers] and vomits yellow pollen. the particles move in the air, winding around one another. i pick my knees. i tear my skin with a razor blade and my muscle aches. golden amber pours out of the devil tree. the fluid streams towards my legs and i stand up on the devil tree root to avoid the fluid. [it will be like our child, the devil tree says] looking at the dusty pollen. i lean over and peel thin sheets of bark up. the devil tree gnashes its roots. [what are you doing, the devil tree asks.] i jump over the syrup river and land on a rounded boulder. [all i need is a piece of skin, i say.] i rap my knuckles on the rock. my bones crush into dirt. the devil tree lashes its branches out and seizes the dusty pollen. the devil tree pulls the particles to its bark and heaving bone fruits drop out of its trunk. red and purple juices saturate the ground. i smell raw sugar. i push my arm down my throat and gag. my throat flexes around the limb. [you are a picture of self-indulgence, the devil tree says. look at you. feeding yourself a fleshy luxury.] the limbs roll across the ground and brush against me. i kick the wooden arms away. [this isn't luxury, i say. this is self-mutilation. because if i have to, i'll carve myself into steaks, then eat the meat raw. self-cannibalism. i don't know if it's possible but i'll try.] the devil tree flexes. [you can self-cannibalize me, the devil tree says.] i dig in the dirt. [it isn't the same, i say.] the dead nun vomits me and i am awake. i am awake.

pink eye orbs

land on the dead nun and pick her dried skin. [you are salty, the
pink eye orbs whisper] and leak large yellow droplets. green
plants sprout from the dead nun's skin. her flesh cracks. the
weeds grow until they cover her face. [she is a flytrap, the pink
eye orbs say. and we do not like that. we resent her meat. bite
the cheeks. make them go. but do we? yes, we must. we must
eat the meat. but with what? we have no mouths!] the pink
eye orbs fling themselves to the ground and stare through the
stones. [what if you chewed the meat, then spit it over our
bodies? then we could indulge in the fluid draining free, the
pink eye orbs say.] i flick my wrists and the pink eye orbs jump.
[not allowed, i say. none of that is allowed. i do not think it
should happen. and if it does, then you will be mauled by a
celestial beast with tiger stripes.] the pink eye orbs lift their
lids off the dirt. [a celestial beast with tiger stripes, they ask.
how is that possible? is it gas or a cat? if it has tiger stripes,
is it a triger? but what if it does not roar?] the pink eye orbs
puncture the ground with their lids. i lift them up and shake
their skin several times. [we understand, they whisper] and sink
to the floor. [it is a tiger, they say. but not a tiger. something
else. a regit? no. a giter? or a getir? an itger.] they nod until their lashes break off at the stems. [how silly of us, the
pink eye orbs whisper.] i climb onto the dead nun's shoulders.
her meat breaks beneath my feet. i push her down. the pink
eye orbs climb onto their respective tombstones. [i left some
friends behind, i say, scaling the tomb cave walls. i should have
been back already. but i'm still here. and getting farther away.
i forgot that i might be hurting them.] my womb cramps. i
double over. the pink eye orbs stare. [what hurts you, they ask.]

they rub their lashes against my face. [my uterus, i say.] i vomit rocks. boulders strike the ground. the pink eye orbs dart away. [too many hard things, they say. how do you have a uterus? we thought you put that away. you shouldn't have anything that isn't made of lace.] i collapse on the ground. the dead nun pulls her cheekbones apart and tucks her chin into her head. [turtle, she grunts. that religious shell should keep growing.] the dead nun sits on the floor. she piles rocks up on her ankle. one by one, the rocks settle on one another. the tower sways from left to right, each twist to the side more dramatic than the last. the dead nun gags. the rocks fall. [i can applaud your flesh, she says.] she stands. her ankles click softly as she walks. the pink eye orbs gather around me. [you will not eat the bloodless girl, they say] and fan their lashes to form a dehydrated hurricane. wind pushes the dead nun back. i grab the lashes in my fists and yank. the pink eye orbs stare. [did we do the wrong thing, they ask.] i nod. the pink eye orbs sigh. [we did wrong, they whisper. again. we always do something wrong. it is our nature.] the pink fades to a dull brick shade. [i have to get back to the skeletal pumpkin, i say.] the dead nun smiles. her face splinters as her mouth curves. [the same direction, the dead nun says. it is the same direction to return to your late pumpkin friend and to touch the blood baths. but you cannot look to your right. it is not allowed.] the dead nun vomits. a pink pumpkin path spreads.

pumpkins cover the
barren lands. i lift the gourds up and set them on the pink
eye orbs until the little eyes drop. they strike the dirt heavily. [why would you hurt us, the pink eye orbs whisper] and
tear their skin open. the rocks drop off their faces. the pink
eye orbs jump into the air and buzz around my face, swat-
ting my cheeks with their lashes until my muscle aches. i push
them away. green threads wind their ways across the dirt. i pick
through the string and find a parsley sprig beneath a rusted
meat hook. the parsley wilts in my hands. i place the parsley
in my mouth and it melts on my tongue, staining the exterior a faded brown-green. my uterus strains against my abdomen. gray skin drops out of my thighs and snakes onto the
floor. the skeletal pumpkin rolls onto the path. [are you coming
back, the pumpkin asks.] the pink eye orbs stare at the curving meat. they lift thin ligaments and hold them in the air until
the meat ferments, coming apart in many strands. [what have
you done to yourself, the pink eye orbs ask.] i exhale sharply
and my hair falls onto my tongue. i choke the strands back
and follicles ball up in my throat. i swallow the hair clot. [i'm
emptying my stomach, i say.] i stumble forward, following the
left-leaning pumpkin road. the pumpkin faces grow until they
gulp my feet. i kick the gourds away. [why aren't you happy to
see me, the skeletal pumpkin whines.] the pink eye orbs hover
above the vegetables. [but you have nothing to force out, the
pink eye orbs say.] they spread their lashes across my stomach.
parsley solids foam in my belly button. they cling to the curved
lip, then fall over, crashing to the floor. parsley shards scatter
everywhere. green points pierce the hard pumpkin shells and
peel the meaty innards. [what have you done, the pink eye orbs

ask. the dead nun never said to kill the vegetables. we are only supposed to follow. you are supposed to follow. but you kill the vegetables. you tear them into pieces. you toss them on the floor to brown around their middles. if the mold starts? do you know what happens then? the faces grow. and spread over the dirt. colonies of gaping mouths. we've seen this before. and the mushroom change hurts.] the pink eye orbs swallow the pumpkin faces whole. [you've pushed us to this, the pink eye orbs shriek. we are murderers now. we tear the pumpkins into pieces. how could you? we didn't want the meat.] the pink eye orbs vomit pumpkin pieces up. i reach for the meat but they fall apart beneath a layer of ocular acid. [aren't caustic substances bad for your eyes, i ask.] the pink eye orbs click their lids. [you are bad for us, they say. you made us leave the hooks.] [you volunteered. you brought me here and stayed, i say.] the pink eye orbs' lashes drop off their lids. individual strands catch a light breeze and waft to the floor. they stack up, one on top of the next, until a tower of lashes hovers over us. [now our hair has turned against us, the pink eye orbs whisper. we are rotten. we have no worth left.] the pink eye orbs crack their surfaces like egg shells. the white separates and a pale yellow glob slips out of the fluid. it shudders on the lens then bursts. sticky strands hang off the gelatin. i hold my hands beneath the fluid and it drips onto my palms. the fluid shines brilliantly and gossamer dust slicks the strands until they snap into several mucus ropes. i take my hands back and dip them into skeletal pumpkin's shell to clean on rough seeds.

later, after the
pumpkin mess has grown new roots and the pink eye orbs
curl up in balls in the dirt to sleep, i dig a shallow grave and
climb inside. my hands press hard against my abdomen. i feel
every hard bulge of cyst jutting out against my skin and the
clots move independently of my flesh. [it could be a calcium
deposit, the skeletal pumpkin whispers in my ear.] it licks the
side of my cheek, tearing the skin open. dust rolls out of the
opening. i arch my back and apply pressure to my lower body.
my uterus aches. it strains against my upper thighs. [you cannot force me out, my uterus says. you need knives to do that.] i
turn my head but there is no skeletal pumpkin. i stare at a thick
dirt wall stretching several inches above my head and i dig my
fingers into the earth, wrenching the crumbling powder down.
my stomach tenses. the cyst grows. my hands drop off my skin
and i look down my torso. the cyst widens. i watch my skin
move with it. the muscle opens and shuts. it looks like a mouth:
all flesh color on the outside and raw red on the inside. [how
can you grow when there's no fluid, i ask.] the cyst swells to the
bottoms of my breasts. i pinch the growth. i pop its top and
dust flows out. i dig my fingers in deeper, bruising my wrists.
dark green blotches cover my arms. the dirt walls move. they
crumble near the edges. [is this the beginning of the blood, i
ask.] i bend at the waist and the cyst bursts out of me. my skin
peels back. it drapes over the dirt floor. the cyst thumps. it beats
softly. the meat edges crack. dust bubbles inside the cyst. i lift
the cyst slightly. the meat slices curdle. they break apart in my
hands. [do not touch, the meat shouts.] the cyst bites. its roots
sink into my hands and tear the flesh up. [are you hungry, the
cyst asks.] it salivates dust. i hold my wounds to my mouth and

lick until my mouth crumbles. [i'm not hungry, i say.] the cyst spreads apart. it breaks into three smaller cysts. [yes, you are, the cysts chorus.] they leap into my veins. clots move up my arteries, tearing the constricted walls. [you must eat, the clots shout] ripping my organs. they lift me. i move slowly, my arms and legs staggering. i climb out of the grave. the pink eye orbs turn in their sleep. [you must eat, the cysts say. a growing girl like you, so dry because you never get enough meat. you have to eat.] the cysts push me into the pink eye orbs. i grab a stone and beat the cysts with the blunt end. rock pieces fall down my stomach. they rain onto the floor and strike the pink eye orbs. [the bloodless girl wakes, the pink eye orbs say] opening their lids. the cysts wrench my mouth open. i vomit dust over the pink eye orbs. their gelatin crusts over. their lids stretch and break. leathery pieces drop to the floor. [it is meat, the cysts shriek.] they force my arms down. my fingers break. i hold the bones but they snap. my fingers curl around the pink eye orbs. they strain against my palms. fleshy lids shove into the marrow. gelatin pours down my hands. [why, the pink eye orbs cry. why?] the cysts force my arms up. the pink eye orbs cover my mouth. lashes stab my tongue. [it isn't me, i cry. i'm not doing this.] the cysts rub my throat. they move slowly, winding their bodies in a clockwise position until i swallow. the pink eye orbs digest. i do not taste them.

i hear bells.

bells and bells and bells. in my stomach. on my skin. bells everywhere. while the pink eye orbs grate against my rotten kidneys. pink eye orb dust. while i cringe. and try to look at the dead trees that have surpassed the wooden state and now live as rocks, flesh hard and heavy with clear crystals. quartz lumps. sapphire stumps. i snap a twig and mica sheets crumble. they dust the pink eye orbs. they shine on the clanking bells. bells get into my lungs so that whenever i breathe, i wheeze bells. i chime against my will. and the pink eye orbs digest against theirs. eventually, the bells quiet and i focus on the pink eye orbs. they churn, their gelatin swelling and smearing, their hard parts sticking to my innards' wall, the liquid bits draining out of my pores. glistening with pale red partially fluid crystals, the pink eye orbs move through my skin, forcing their lashes through my veins, their gelatin drying into obscure spider formations and each is stranger than the last because the legs twist to the wrong sides, then grow out of the same pores before braiding around one another. my muscles hum but stay static. the pink eye orbs flutter. lenses separate from corneas separate from irises separate from pupils separate from retinas separate separate separate. until i force my fingers between them and drag them together. but they do not stay in position. they bump against one another, then slide away, flesh sagging until it puddles up on my bone surfaces. [this is the most fluid i have had in lifetimes, i say] and the cysts slash the pink eye orbs into pieces. [none of this fluid is yours, the cysts hum and clang bells in my ears until my ears deafen.] the bells start again. they thrash against my cheeks. they move in my eyes, silver bells and brass bells and iron bells. brash bells, all stomping against me until my solid blood melts into a dusty residue. cysts move up my neck and cluster in my brain. their weaving fibers move in circles, painting the back of my head blue and yellow. [i don't want colors, i say] and slap the cysts. the cysts duck into my brain matter. my palm hits my cranial matter and the gray flesh rots on contact. i swallow hard. the cysts slide out of the wrinkles. [not too bright, they whisper. you can't get rid of us. you need a knife for that. and you don't have one. teeth don't count.] pink eye orbs cross my tongue. they settle on my teeth, then drop into the tiny cracks. [help us, they squeal] and disappear into my gum line. i push my nails into my teeth. my fingers stretch and grind. the cysts stack my brain flesh over their bodies. [you can't get them out. they're dust now. that's what you have under there. dust factories. stacks of solid matter, cremated without your permission. it's sad. but you did this to yourself. do you remember the salt days, the cysts ask.] they bite my brain. my spleen squeals. it wrenches around on its stalk and bites the abdominal wall closest to its mouth. the skeletal pumpkin reaches a fingerling stem into my ear and stabs the cysts with a knife made of bone fruit seeds. pink eye orbs spill out of the wounds. they cluster around my stomach entrance. they pulse. i press my hands against them. i push them back in. [if i can keep you inside, then i can protect you, i say.] the pink eye orbs slip past my fingers. they fall in the dirt. [you ate us. we've been digested. there is no protecting us now, the pink eye orbs whisper] and slide, dripping.

the cysts die.

they die slowly and then they die quickly and soon enough, there are no cysts at all and i am alone on the graveyard floor, pulling hair out of the dirt and wrapping the strands around my knees. i wish i could cut the circulation off but there is no blood flow to interrupt. so i sit quietly, playing with the hair until my skin snags and rips. [you should walk, the dirt says.] the dirt opens. the dirt spreads into a red pathway leading upward. i step onto the path and walk slowly. dirt crunches beneath my feet so loudly, it sounds like porcine squealing. i cover my ears. the dirt becomes fluid. it runs beneath my soles. the liquid pulls me down. i tense my legs and force my way forward. [how long are you going to stay like this, i ask.] the mud smooths again. it hardens. the dirt becomes rocks that lead onto the road. the barren lands end. trees sprout slowly, beginning as stubs, then expanding into large bushes. the trees reach into the road and press against my arms. [mother, they whisper. are you mother?] the trees shrink back. tiny eyes roll down the trunks and burrow into dirt piled on the roots. i step off the road and stand on the roots. i shove my arms into the dirt and root around. gelatin brushes over my fingers. it clings to my fingernails. i lift my hands and the eyes drop off my fingertips. they fall into the sandy ground. [you've finally arrived, a voice says.] i turn around. fog moves up the road, obscuring the ground. i squint my eyes. [damn this fog, the voice says] and a pale hand swats the fog away. i step onto the road and the hand reaches for my face. [don't touch me, i say. i don't know you.] the hand drops. [sorry, dear, the voice says. my manners are terrible at times. now, now. come here.] an arm breaks the fog up. an old woman with bright green eyes and a heart-shaped face steps forward.

her gray dress sweeps over the road, gathering concrete and pebbles in the fraying hem. the old woman clutches her smooth hands together and cracks her fingers. bone bubbles push out of her knuckles. i stare at the joints and the old woman flattens them down. her wide mouth spreads into a smile that drips down her chin. [i've been waiting for you, the old woman says. i am BABA. you may call me BABA. come to my BABA house.] she curls her fingers around my wrists and yanks. the old woman turns her head and runs forward, her eyes running with red fluid. [my innards are festive, the old woman says. so festive. they love holidays. and it's always a holiday in the woods. now come along. the house is getting cold.] the fog sags to the ground. it dissolves into water. the old woman thrashes the mist with her toenails. [to the bend, BABA says] and points around the road corner. i lean hard to the left. BABA squeals. [i like you, she cries] and pulls me onto her shoulders. my fingers fasten beneath her chin. BABA runs, her ankles cracking beneath our weight. her stomach flops up and down, then slams against a tree, cracking the trunk in half. i close my eyes. my hair bounces. my eyes hurt. i grit my teeth and the enamel weakens. [the house, the old woman says] and lets me go. i slide off her back and onto the floor. she points between her legs. i stare at her swollen abdomen. [not that, my dear, BABA says.] i look past her knees. a brick house smokes behind her. its skeletal face flashes.

the BABA woman

tucks me into a large straw bed. she drags a heavy sheet over my chest and forces the blanket under my arms. BABA steps away from the bed and scratches the wooden walls. a tiny egg in the corner hatches. an orange fire spills out of the egg and burns through the floor. [oh good, the eggs are done, BABA says and claps her thighs together.] BABA hums. she gets on her knees and reaches beneath the bed. her hands press against the mattress' underside. her fingers push into my back. i cringe. my spine twists. [here it is, BABA shouts.] she pulls her arms back and waves a tiny meat candle in the air. [did you need extra light, i ask.] the candle wick touches the bottom of my nose. i smell meat. my stomach growls. BABA pulls the candle away. a black dot drips down her lip and settles just below her mouth. she smiles wildly and the droplet glimmers. [do you have liquid, i ask] and BABA's tongue darts out of her mouth. the tip touches the droplet and absorbs it. her meat blackens, then turns red again. BABA clears her throat. the skin rises and falls around the top of her chest. the meat odor sharpens. BABA's smile widens until her cheekbones break. [are you hungry, she asks.] another droplet falls. her tongue snakes around her jaws and catches the drip. her teeth crack down the center. [you never told me if you have fluid, i say.] BABA lowers the candle to the floor. the meat fumes cover my face. i choke them down. [of course i don't have any fluids, she says. i'm as dry as you are.] her bones crack. [i was the bloodless girl first, she says. but then i grew into the BABA woman. but i still don't have any fluids.] she lifts the candle quickly. the wick strokes the bottom of her chin and cooks the skin. [eeeee, she squeals] and cups her free hand to the burned meat. BABA backs away.

[so sorry. i have to get dinner ready. sleep, my dear. rest, she says.] she turns and rushes to the door. it opens on its own and BABA darts through. the door slams. her footsteps echo around the house. i push the blankets down. they scratch my knees. red marks cover my skin. i lean off the bed and run my hands over the floor. wax covers the ground. i slide my palms in a slow circle, feeling the wood grain and individual nailheads. my fingers brush over a cold patch. i lean farther and my fingers slip. liquid. there is liquid on the floor. i sit up. the fireplace grows until the light covers a wall. i step off the bed and walk to the fireplace. heat burns my skin. i flinch. i squint and watch the flames closely. they separate and a white coal piece bursts out of the spaces. i force my hands into the fire and scrape the flames' outer surface. but the fire flesh doesn't burn. it peels apart like wallpaper. i scratch and the fire curls in tight rolls. they drop to the floor and sound like parchment paper, dry sheets rustling softly. i press my lips together. i press my hands flat against the flames and push. the paper crumbles. it drops to the floor, orange ash glowing. i step over. [i hope you're resting well, the BABA woman shouts from inside the walls.] a metal spoon clanks against a thick-lipped bowl. she slurps something. [in the morning, i will show you the liver fields, she says] and swallows. her thick phlegm moves in her throat. a door made of silver filigree stands in front of my bed.

liver fields reek

of unprocessed fecal matter. i stand behind the BABA woman while she breathes the fermented air. [liver is the best meat, the BABA woman says. i like it in sausages. and chopped up. maybe even sautéed with a bit of onion. it is wondrous. like compound butter mixed with marrow and chives.] she turns around, her eyes glistening with tears. the BABA woman wipes her face quickly, rubbing the tears away. [would you like a piece, she asks] and whips a machete out of her side. she snags a liver branch and cuts the stem. the liver falls into her engorged lap. she pushes the machete into her dress and throws the liver at me. i bat it away. [i'd rather not, i say. i try not to eat meat if i can help it.] the BABA woman forces the meat between her jaws. it squishes. meat juice dribbles down her face. red stains her skin. i grimace. [how can you touch fluids if you're blood-less, i ask. just looking at fluid can make me sick.] the BABA woman stares at her bloody hands. she places them against her mouth and licks the fingers individually. [only meat, my dear, she says. you think you'll get sick if you eat it. but you won't. you should try it.] she cuts another liver. the liver branches sway gently. their skin squeaks with the movement. glossy peels re-flect our faces. i play with the tip of my tongue, forcing my nails into the skin and pulling to the right. the BABA woman puts the cut liver into her throat. her mouth stays wide open. [i should have known better, she says. the meat. it isn't always as ripe as it should be. sometimes, it tastes like solid blood. or mayonnaise. my stomach clenches for some fat.] she runs the machete over her tongue, licking the blood off. [how can you really lick without the saliva, i ask.] the BABA woman lowers the machete. she sighs loudly. the liver trees hum with her. [i drink water, she says. i am bloodless but never deny myself fluid. so i let the water settle in my mouth until it makes a faux saliva i can manage to store beneath my tongue. i secrete as needed. and it makes the food taste better. especially the livers. they get extra meat. and i cry because they are so delicious.] she wipes her eyes again. water drips out of her hands. droplets strike the dirt and the livers swell until their casings burst. raw liver meat hangs from the weakening trees until the meat falls apart, ground piece by ground piece. the BABA woman gets on her knees beneath the trees and turns her head up. she catches the flesh on her tongue. [so lovely, she says. i've never tasted anything so wonderful. it makes my stomach tremble. i can taste the meat in all its glory. the heart steaks. the liver shakes. oh, can't you have some?] she slaps her tongue around and partially digested meat drops off the edges. the meat falls into the dirt and rolls around several times until it looks like a fried croquette. [have a bite, the BABA woman says again.] she lifts the fried ball and waves it in front of my mouth. a strong liver scent settles on the back of my tongue. i swallow and the dry air leaves an acidic feeling in the center of my chest. i press my lips together. the BABA woman flinches. she thrusts the ground meat at me. meaty pieces drop. [i'm so tired, i say. the sky seems much lower today.] i swipe my wrist across my head. the BABA woman swallows the liver ball.

i return to

the silver doorway. the BABA woman walks downstairs, her
feet scraping over the uneven floor and causing splinters. i
rap on the doorway. i lean into it but it does not open. i push
the doorway down. it eases its way onto the ground, moving like fluid, and the silver is like fresh water, but i do not
touch it. i do not touch the silver until it is solid again. i sit
on the doorway. i pull the doorknob and it slips out of my
grasp. [how do i get you open, i ask.] i press against my stomach. the pink eye orb remnants squeeze out of my belly button. [what have you done, the remnants ask. you burned the
walls. you took the doorway. she will eat you, boil your bones
for soup, then slurp you until you hurt. why did you find the
door?] the pink eye orb remnants drill holes into my skin.
they squeeze their lashed bodies out of the openings. my skin
puckers around them. it grows, then shrinks down as the pink
eye orb remnants yank free of the sucker holes. their bodies
strike the floor. pink eyes splinter. their dusty bodies smash
apart. i touch the door frame gently. i stroke the filigree. my
fingertips prod the lacy edging, reaching in and out of the tiny
holes, pulling curled flowers apart. [my heart beats, my heart
does not beat, my heart beats, my heart does not beat, my
heart beats, my heart does not beat, the pink eye orb powder
recites] while i throw the petals down. the petals clank against
the wood. [i cry terribly, i do not cry terribly, i cry terribly, i
do not, the pink eye orb powder screams. i cry terribly! i cry
terribly! but i do not!] the powder drains into the floorboard
cracks. the dust in a waterfall motion. it fills a small tidal pool
beneath the floor. i put my eye to the crack. [how do i get
through, i ask.] the pink eye orb powder trembles. it shakes

and scatters. [just blow, they cry. it's good. it tastes like liquid air. just blow and the floorboards will just rip apart.] the pink eye orb dust piles in a small mound. i raise my head. [i meant, how do i get the door open, i say.] i lie flat on the doorway, aligning my heart with the knob. [if this won't open it, then i guess i'll just have to ingest the metal and hope for the best, i say.] i swallow my tongue. it worms its way through my chest, poking my heart and prodding the dead organs into a mechanical sort of motion. metallic ligaments strain. they squeak from lack of biological lubricant. the stitches snap apart. the bones click. i tremble. my stomach drops. [stop it, i hiss at my limbs.] my stomach drops again. the doorknob pushes hard against my chest, staining the breast meat dark blue-brown. i inhale. my stomach drops with the door. the silver swings inward, smacking against an unseen wall. i brace my arms and legs on the door frame and hover over the space. a pair of leather wings juts out of the doorway. the skin cuts the length of my chest. i arch my spine, then contract, drawing my stomach inward. [you can't mutilate me before supper, i say.] i raise one leg and kick the wings. the beast squeals. it slams its wings together, then spins on its ball joints to face me. red eyes glare at me. goat milk pours out of the red. [what are you doing up there, the BABA woman shouts. come down for dinner.] fire locks on the bedroom door roast. i crawl into the space. i do not brush the spiked walls.

spiked walls slope
downward for many miles, while i fall alongside of them, my
limbs tucked into my torso for protection. bells chime inside
the walls and bite my lower lip until the skin breaks. dust dribbles out. powder covers the outer wound. it thins and spreads
across my mouth. i lick the dust and my mouth twitches with
an anesthetized reaction. the floor rises and strikes me. i hit
hard and my bones crack. i grunt. my body aches. i move slowly, unwinding my arms and legs, lifting my back up. i arch and
bend forward. [it is time for dinner, the BABA woman shouts.
where are you?] i hear her behind the spiked walls, walking in
circles, her bloated face heaving and smashing against door
frames. wood and plaster splinter. i stand slowly, my joints seiz-
ing, bone marrow crumbling. the walls reach into the domestic
sky and i watch their tapered progression upward. at their bottom, tucked halfway into the spikes, is a tiny glass doorway.
i lean forward and knock three times. the glass echoes. a girl
stares back at me. she pouts slightly and her mauve-colored lips
pucker. the girl lifts a piece of raw meat and saws it in half with
her angled cheekbones. the meat divides in two before she fin-
ishes the first downward stroke. her eyes flash bright turquoise
and long dark hair settles around her gray shoulders. [who are
you, i ask] and the girl sticks her tongue out. the tongue tip is
uneven. i reach out. a leather wing smacks my hand away. [don't
touch her, the wing says.] i turn. a black boulder stands close
to me, bony wings wrapped in cured meat jutting out of its
rounded back. [why not, i ask.] the black boulder's wings flap
lazily. the wings lift up, meet in the air, and slump. [because she
isn't a real person, the wings say. she's an imaginative figment,
a creativity fiber. something of that nature.] the boulder turns

in a circle. rock opens into a goat-like face. my eyes widen and i jump back, hitting the glass doorway with my hip. the goat rock creature sighs. [terrible mistake, it says. now the doorway eats you.] glass shards bite my leg. the girl crawls out of the doorway, her body stretching until it is almost serpentine. she wraps her torso around my knee and bites. i smack her face. her eyes melt. they pour down my leg, aqua rivulets streaming across my skin and into the dirt. my leg burns. [let go, i cry.] i punch her melted eyes. her mouth crunches. her lips drop off her meat and strike the floor. the goat creature's wings dart forward and inhale the glass. [is it glass or meat, i scream.] the goat creature stretches its back. its vertebrae crack. [something like both, it says.] long talons drop out of its stomach and scratch the floor. the girl squeezes her body tighter. i gasp and my chest burns with respiratory rawness. i pull her hair until the strands snap. her scalp stretches and tears. glassy blood pours from the opening. it soaks my skin. [no, no, i cry.] i lean away from her and grab a rock. i beat her face with the small stone. glass shatters. the girl's skin crashes. fangs leave my skin. i stand in a pile of broken glass. [come along, the goat thing says] gesturing at a tunnel. i stare at the shattered glass. [who was that, i ask.] the goat creature rolls its crystal eyes. [have you ever seen your reflection before, it asks.] i shake my head. [you, it says.]

i follow the

goat creature down a spiraling tunnel filled with heavy rocks and too many pieces of rotten skin. [what should i call you, i ask] bumping into the goat creature's back and knocking it off balance. its wings strike the ceiling above and rocks rain onto our heads. dust rises to the surface of my bruises. [my stomach cramps, i say.] the goat creature touches the ground. it extends its tongue and swipes it over the concrete pathway. [call me the JERSEY DEVIL, the goat creature says] and shakes its shoulders until its wings come loose. the wings fall to the floor. they melt around their centers, the edges curling until they drip down the bones. i step over the wings. [don't you need those, i ask.] the JERSEY DEVIL walks on. [i can grow more, it says. i regenerate flying apparatuses spontaneously. come along.] the JERSEY DEVIL turns three corners. [how did my reflection come alive, i ask.] the JERSEY DEVIL sighs. [you ask too many questions, it says. but your reflection came alive because the glass is magical. like an onion. many layers, each peeled back from the core, capable of standing alone. and you touched the center, waking up the soul.] the JERSEY DEVIL nods. i narrow my eyes. i push my finger into the monster's side and it yelps. its head strikes the ceiling again. the stone shatters and a small indentation breaks in the ceiling. [that makes no sense, i say.] the JERSEY DEVIL sighs. [no one said it had to make sense, the JERSEY DEVIL says. i never said it and neither did you. it was a mirror in the BABA woman's house. and it came alive. you can do the same thing with candlelight and misery. or an ax. it depends. do you like your metal wet or bloody?] the JERSEY DEVIL wriggles its eyebrows up and down. [there isn't an option for metal being dry, i ask.] [then the spells would never work, the JERSEY DEVIL says.] it stops walking. i walk into its back and bounce away. my back hits the opposite wall and a loose spike pushes into my skin. i gasp. dust flows out of the cut. the JERSEY DEVIL turns around. [i touched the spiked wall. i whisper.] the JERSEY DEVIL shrugs. it points at the floor. i look down and several yellowing bones stare up at me. [they all touched the spikes, too. what's the problem, the JERSEY DEVIL asks.] [they're dead, i cry.] [aren't we all, the JERSEY DEVIL asks.] it lifts a bone and pushes it into its pig snout. the goat face twists and mashes together. the meat curdles around the lips and falls onto the back of the tongue. the walls rumble. the JERSEY DEVIL glances up. it touches the ceiling. [oh, it says] and places its hooked claws under its neck. the JERSEY DEVIL sighs loudly. the walls shake and stones loosen. they roll over my feet, pinning me in place. [what's happening, i cry. are we going to die in here? the walls are falling apart.] the JERSEY DEVIL backs away. the walls break. the BABA woman pushes through, swinging her ax tongue in the air. she swipes the blade at me and i push into the wall. pointed spikes stick into my skin. i bleed and the rancid fluid runs down my spine. [you thought you could come into my house and take my son away, the BABA woman screams. harlot! whore! how dare you?] i turn my head. she moves the ax. the JERSEY DEVIL sprouts concrete wings and flies away.

the BABA woman

tries to cut me. she screams into stone walls. spikes fall to the
floor. they touch the rock bottom and tinkle loudly, like falling
glass. [so you touched the walls, she says. weren't you warned
away from the sharp points?] the BABA woman drops her ax.
the blade clatters on the floor. it stops near my ankles. i keep
my hands flat against the wall. the BABA woman screams.
[how dare you, she asks. i tried to feed you. i brought you here
so you could have a good dinner. and you open a doorway into
my basement. you chase my precious progeny away? how will
i live without my son? i love him. he doesn't belong out there.]
the BABA woman tears her fleshy chin apart. raw meat splatters the ground. i hold my breath. i smell rancid blood. i gag. a
digestive pressure rises into my throat. i gag again. dust settles
in the center of my neck. i press my lips together and breathe
through my nose. [do not vomit, i whisper. do not vomit.] but
my lips part. dusty vomit spews out of my mouth. it covers the
front of my shirt and streams onto the floor. the BABA woman watches the vomit. [wonderful, she screams. now i have to
clean my vaginal canals.] the BABA woman raises a horsehair
brush in the air and scrubs the stone ceiling. [but the floor is
dirty, i say.] the BABA woman throws the brush at me. [so
you think you can insult my cleaning habits, she asks. i've been
keeping my son clean for longer than you've known him. you
presume to know that i am dirty. because you've seen my liver
fields and think badly about any woman who has a love for organs. but i am not sick. and i am not wrong. i am just a woman
who wants to have some liver several times a day, cooked in
a variety of forms. you refused to eat any of that meat. you
wouldn't even put it near your mouth. you just stared at the

muscle and looked down on me. you think you're better than i am, because you're bloodless.] the BABA woman punches the walls. the walls shake. dead wings fall out of the ceiling. they drop onto our heads, knocking us to the floor. i lie in my fleshy vomit. i move the dust around with my fingertips until it swirls into a DNA design. the BABA woman gets onto her knees. she pushes herself out of the vomit puddle and twists her mouth until it obscures her eyes. [i am a good mother, she cries. i am a wonderful mother. i gave birth to my JERSEY DEVIL without complaint. the man with the bag over his head told me that the birth would be painful but i did what was necessary. i did what a mother should. i pushed him out and gave him skin. i let him drink until my bones were completely dry. because i loved him. so i went bloodless for a moment but the juices came back. and then i was better again. then i was made of meat again. but you. you have nothing inside. just dust. how did you get that way? i want to be like you.] she catches my face between her hands and squeezes. [how did you get to be bloodless, she asks. just tell me. i'll drain everything out into a copper tub if you tell me.] my uterus rattles. she plunges her fingertips into my belly button. she tears my skin apart and grasps my womb tightly in her fingertips. she twists the womb to one side, ripping it off its stem. thorny wings jut out of the walls. they cut her face in half.

the JERSEY DEVIL

strings the BABA woman up by her knees. her double faces
rip apart. rancid tongue meat pours out of her throat. a strong
blood smell fills the air. the JERSEY DEVIL pulls bones out
of its teeth and tosses them away. [what good is calcium when
it lacks marrow, the JERSEY DEVIL asks.] the BABA woman,
half-dead and flowing, reaches for my knees. [i will kill you,
she hisses. i will wear you like a rope necklace. i will rip you
into pieces like a flower.] her eyes wobble around her head.
the BABA woman yanks her teeth out and throws them at me.
enamel pieces strike my sides and bite my ribs. i pluck little
hairs off her face. the BABA woman foams. each hair strand
ends in a tiny claw hook. [give them back, she shrieks] thrash-
ing the chains. the JERSEY DEVIL lifts me by the back of
my neck. [you have to go now, it says. we need to go together.]
the JERSEY DEVIL flings me onto its back. i fall between
its wings. the wings settle against the JERSEY DEVIL's back.
they flatten me. i sit up and the wings knock me down again.
the JERSEY DEVIL's back is moldy. orange turnips sprout
out of the leather muscle. candlestick shapes protrude from
the tops. i pluck a turnip and strip its hairy meat off. the
JERSEY DEVIL rears up. it shrieks. [why would you peel me,
it screams] and the wings pull the turnip out of my hands. i
reach for the root vegetable. it clatters down the tunnel. the
BABA woman strains for it. her back stretches until the meat
thins. ligaments snap quickly, sounding like interrupted musical
chords. the BABA woman twists at the waist. she knocks her
head against the spiked wall. [i will get you, she says.] blood fills
her teeth. she spits several mouthfuls out. [wicked little thing.
i will get you, the BABA woman cries.] i dig my fingers into

the JERSEY DEVIL's back. it lifts off the ground. the BABA woman snaps her teeth at its hoofs. [i am your mother. love me, she screams.] the JERSEY DEVIL bats its mother's head with the tiny fangs protruding from its rocky lips. the hooks snag her face and tear the flesh. her double mouths move frantically, working around an invisible piece of meat. i duck down. wings cover me. they catch the BABA woman's digestive gases and coast down the tunnel, leathery meat flapping with the air currents. striated rocks pass our heads. the JERSEY DEVIL ducks low. it smashes the rocks with its anvil-like tail. the JERSEY DEVIL's skin is cold. i shiver as the temperature leaks into my clothing. blue patches cover my skin. [i am so cold, i whisper.] the JERSEY DEVIL knocks the ceiling apart with its head. rocks roll down the wings and fill the tunnel. the JERSEY DEVIL clings to the rock walls with its tail and claws. it climbs upward. the wings cradle me. [we'll be at the sun soon enough, the JERSEY DEVIL says.] it spits white foam onto the ground. the rocks bubble. they burst and tiny pebbles hit the BABA woman in the face. [she was your mother, i cry. how can you kill her?] the JERSEY DEVIL pulls its body out of the hole. it rolls over the edge and flops onto its side. i climb off its back. the wings fold down. [she ate my stomach folds, the JERSEY DEVIL whispers.] it drops its head. i bend over its side. i stare at its stomach. but there is no stomach. there is only rotten meat, half-chewed, all discolored.

i vomit a

needle and thread. the JERSEY DEVIL stares at me. its crystal eyes shimmer like diamonds. i thread the needle and tear a length of thread. [this will hurt, i say.] the JERSEY DEVIL twists its head all the way around. i stare at the raw stitch marks. yellow and white flesh pushes out of the stitch spaces. liquid fat drips into the mud. [you're done, i say.] the JERSEY DEVIL twists until standing up on its thighs. it pushes its body up the rest of the way and sighs. it looks up. the sky is already dark blue with tiny yellow splashes near the horizon. i grunt softly and step forward. [what do we do, the JERSEY DEVIL asks.] i stare at the veins crossing my wrists. blue and red threads intertwine, then pull apart. they grow up my fingers and cluster near my nail bed. i put my nails in my mouth and bite the crescents off. [you said you saw the road curve ahead, i ask.] the JERSEY DEVIL nods. [it curved to the left for several miles. there were more than thirty turns, one right after the next. but none of it looked like a circle, the JERSEY DEVIL says.] i look down the shadowed road. [then we'll follow it, i say. it might lead us back to the devil tree.] the JERSEY DEVIL plods forward, boulder body shaking. i cling to its spine and follow.

halfway down the
curved road, my skin goes bad. rancid around the edges, moldy towards the middle, the skin darkens and peels off my bones. [can you mold if there's no moisture, the JERSEY DEVIL asks] and picks its teeth with a suicide branch. dead skin hangs onto the end. my arms feel heavy. they hang down my waist and the loose skin resembles a skirt wrapped around my bones. [are all your parts female, the JERSEY DEVIL asks.] but i cannot answer it. i swallow my tongue. i chew the meat. the JERSEY DEVIL plays with its hollow jaws. [i knew a woman once, the JERSEY DEVIL whispers. she lived in a shed. and when she was tired, she would scream until the walls melted into her mouth. then the wood hardened again and her tongue stayed stretched flat. it was beautiful. the world's first living wood woman. i ate her. but that was later. when the wood lost its clear lacquer and she started splintering.] i sit in the middle of the road. [it's not safe, the JERSEY DEVIL cries.] it moves its tiny hands up and down in the air. but i am sick. i lower myself onto my side. the hard road bruises my side. tiny stones stick into my skin and roll around beneath my bones, pushing up so hard that my arteries become bright blue splotches. [i am in such pain, i say.] the JERSEY DEVIL lifts me by the waist. i dangle in the air, my eyes filled with red dust. [what if i vacuum you, the JERSEY DEVIL asks.] it shows me its vortex-like tongue. the muscle whips in the air, stirring air currents until they fall apart. i stare at the stones. [we have to keep going, i say.] i push myself to my feet. the JERSEY DEVIL walks slowly. its stomach meat pulls against the stitches but they hold tightly. i hold my arms against my chest and breathe slowly. [all curved roads lead back home, i whisper. all curved roads.] meat

drops off my bones. the bruises spread. dust spills out. it leaves a red and yellow trail behind me. i step to the left and the dust follows. i turn to the right and the dust turns as well. [it hurts, i whisper.] the JERSEY DEVIL lowers itself to the road. [then sit on my back, the JERSEY DEVIL says. i'll carry you back.] its spinal cord shakes. the vertebrae snap into many tiny bones. butter-shaped marrow logs loosen in the bones and slide down the scaled side. fat slicks the road. tiny men wearing leaf faces walk through the puddles. they slip on the slick gravel and fall head-first into the puddle. [scoop them out, i say.] the JERSEY DEVIL stares at the little men. [no, the JERSEY DEVIL says. those little men are no good. they wilt. you store them in vinegar. but then your house smells.] the JERSEY DEVIL steps over them. i stumble. i bump into the JERSEY DEVIL's meat and bounce back. the meat weakens. it splatters my bones. it drips to the floor, long strands pulling and tugging, then snapping near the end. the meat falls, red droplet by scarlet chunk. we turn one corner then the next, and each revolution is given another fresh red mark. [do you need more dust, the JERSEY DEVIL asks. do you need something to eat? eat what you have to from me.] it points at its stitched stomach. [i'm okay, i say.] i breathe deeply and walk again. another corner. another corner. i spit up dust. [...that universal mystery, that girl we love, voices sing. the bloodless girl. the bloodless girl...]

i went rotten

only once before. it was in the blood times, before the skeletal pumpkin pulled me from underground and called me blood-less. the blood times were simple. i was thirsty then. i drank everything and each beverage had to be red. blood droplets in a cup of fresh milk. blood in my water gallons. blood in a vat of chicken soup. blood blood blood. it had to be blood or else i would not eat. and the worm mother cooked what was necessary. she took her afterbirth and dipped it into boiled wa-ter, then used the condensed pigmentation as a bloody food dye. she stabbed the siblings' throats with copper forks so that blood came out of four aligned holes, each wider than the last, so that the blood flow had different grades. the first hole was the worst blood because it was rich with oxygen. the second and third were better because the oxygen was dissipating and the arteries were meant solely for blood again. and the fourth hole, the most beautiful hole of all, had never known oxygen before, so the blood was thick and rich and dark. it was my favorite. i collected the blood in a vat stored in the back of the refrigerator to stay fresh. every day i allowed myself to have a single tablespoon of the blood and the sanguine fluid coated the spoon so thickly, it took five minutes of licking to get the red off. sometimes the flavor was so strong, i couldn't tell the difference between the blood and the copper fork. they tast-ed similar but the copper had a sharper tang than the blood, which was similar to dry wine. so i had some blood, then i had more blood, and finally near the end, i drank from my wrists while the mother worm watched, salt crystals rolling towards her. she cried and her fluid came out of my eyes. i bled her menstruation. i bled for the walls. plaster fluid leaked from my nose. i tore my scalp open, picking the brain matter, and the mother worm cringed as my fingers raked over my scalp, making a harsh [scratch scratch] against the bony skin. the mother worm curled into a tight coil and her skin read: you will die. then she pitched onto her side and stayed still, her wet skin bubbling with prolonged pregnancy as my many siblings bit free of her extensive womb. i ate them. it is shameful but i ate them without tasting. i bit through their throats and sucked their blood like a vampire. blood grew in my neck. blood swelled in my chest. blood poured from the siblings and onto my tongue. then blood flowed out of the mother worm and drowned the kitchen in red fluid. the red stopped. eventually, it faded to a pale pink, then became clear. then the blood was gone and gray ash fell out of the wounds. the ash fell on my head. it soaked my fluids up. i turned my head away but the ash settled on my skin and forced the fluid up my pores. ash thickened to charcoal mud. i stuck my tongue out and ash fell on the saliva. it sucked liquid out of my tongue and the muscle stiffened. i opened my mouth and my jaws cracked. ash smeared across my hands. it covered the floor, sucking blood up, and replacing the moisture with dry powder. i peeled floor tiles up and stacked them in a tower. and dust still poured. it covered my legs. it pushed into my skin and collected in my torso, drying everything. i cried. tears dripped out but they dried. they spilled ash. dust smeared my cheeks. i touched the powder and i was dry. i was dry.

the skeletal pumpkin
stands in the center of the road. it waves its orange arms at me.
[you came back, the skeletal pumpkin sobs. we were waiting
for years.] i step away from the JERSEY DEVIL's splintered
sides and pat the skeletal pumpkin's head. [i was only gone for
three days, i say.] the skeletal pumpkin frowns. it looks at the
dirt road, then lifts its eyes. [did i grow yellow pumpkin blossoms in your absence, the skeletal pumpkin asks.] i shake my
head. the skeletal pumpkin rattles its roots. dry wood shakes
like a drum of beads. [oh, the skeletal pumpkin says. i see. well,
that is good. i wanted you to see what it looks like when the
yellow pumpkin blossoms sprout. they're lovely. there should
be festivals devoted to their honor but no one loves gourds
to that extent. it's so cruel.] the skeletal pumpkin rolls on the
floor. it bumps against my leg and whines loudly. [i thought
you wouldn't come back. i thought you had forgotten about
us. i missed you so much. the devil tree and i missed you. but
you're here. will that thing stay here forever, the skeletal pumpkin whispers.] it points around me at the JERSEY DEVIL. the
monster drops its scaled head. its crystal eyes shine. [i can't go
back to the BABA woman. she's hungry. she'll eat me again,
the JERSEY DEVIL whispers.] it opens its mouth slightly and
fluid runs down its teeth. saliva puddles up on the ground.
the skeletal pumpkin sighs. its hollowed eyes stretch open until
its mouth cracks. orange meat drops out of the hollow. tiny
threads move through the meat. their yellow bodies stand out
against the pumpkin orange flesh. [does it have to stay, the
skeletal pumpkin asks.] i pat the pumpkin head. [yes, i say. it
ate its old mother for me.] the devil tree picks its roots up
and crosses the field. it digs in the dirt. brown powder flies

in the air. the JERSEY DEVIL opens its mouth and sucks the airborne dirt up. [i have never eaten such lovely earth, the JERSEY DEVIL says.] it parts its heavy lips in a strained grin. the devil tree shakes. [i will snap you in half, the devil tree says. what are you doing here?] the devil tree's hanging limb swings in the air. the JERSEY DEVIL drops to the floor and rests its stitched stomach in a mud puddle. [we are radioactive, the skeletal pumpkin shouts. watch us glow in the evening light.] i frown. the skeletal pumpkin's eyes roll around its head. it pauses with its pupils near its stem and squints. [are you nice, the skeletal pumpkin asks.] the JERSEY DEVIL cries. [i am a monster, it shouts.] i pat the JERSEY DEVIL's sides until the monster breathes airy saliva. [they are very mean, the JERSEY DEVIL whispers.] i lean into the scales. [they don't mean to be. they're protective, i say.] the JERSEY DEVIL whimpers. i turn to the skeletal pumpkin and the devil tree. [you have to be nice to him, i say. he isn't a bad monster.] the skeletal pumpkin touches my knees. [where do we go, it asks.] the devil tree lifts off the ground and stands on its root tips. [yes. where do we go, it asks.] the JERSEY DEVIL swings its head in my direction and stares at the horizon. [where do we go, it asks.] the three creatures stare at me. i look at the ground. i glance at the sky. a red streak crosses the devil tree's branches. it pulses brightly. [we're going to find the slaughter place, i say. and then i'll bathe in the blood-filled aluminum tub.]

hungry stone virgins
cross the field in front of the JERSEY DEVIL and bite its tail.
bovine-faced stick figures sprout. the stone virgins clap their
mantle heads together. [there, they whisper. there. we thought
we would never have our blood again. after all, you stole it
from us, bloodless girl. you stole our blood and left us dry. why
would you do that? why would you take our blood and dry us?
we know what you did to the mother worm. or, we know what
the mother worm did to you. poor, bloodless little girl. has the
hooked god accepted you?] the stone virgins pull their religious hoods around their faces until they are dull eyes peering
out of the cloth shadows. [we found the chain to our desires,
the stone virgins whimper] and lick their concrete palms until
pebbles drop out of their mouths. they drop to the floor and
tear the grass up. green blades float in the air. they rain down
on stone virgins' shoulders and the gravel turns verdant. the
stone virgins grind their teeth. [we've seen you watching us,
bloodless girl, they say. we've seen you nailing your hands to
our cloaks. you should settle down and pray. we worry about
you. and wait until we offer our spontaneous births as a sacrifice to the mother worm. all the stone virgins want the mother
worm's likeness. for she, amongst all worms, simply split in
half and removed a daughter. the hooked god carved her skin
and she was pregnant with the dusty savior. as we all should
be. as we pray to be. ah, the fertility that gives our life new
meaning. amen.] the JERSEY DEVIL whips the women away
from its backside. the stone virgins cartwheel through the dry
grass. they spin relentlessly until their skin falls off. [we have
done some terribly broken things to our religious artifacts, the
stone virgins whisper] and grab the bovine-faced men in their

little stone hands. they tear the monsters apart. stones fall to the dirt and leave deep indentations in the terrain. i close my eyes. i breathe in slowly and a rich blood smell travels through the air. it moves around me. it smears red fluid around my eyes and i reach into the deep concave, scooping blood out before it hardens into a thick red coat. [can we eat these statues, the skeletal pumpkin asks] running around the JERSEY DEVIL's goat legs. the JERSEY DEVIL brings one leg down on the skeletal pumpkin's head and holds the gourd in place. stone virgins lift their hands to the heavens and tear the clouds down. they push the fog into their mouths and bite. dark rain pours out of their lips. it flows to the ground, muddying the dirt and staining the bottom rocks. [but i want to eat them, the skeletal pumpkin cries] and gropes its eyes with its roots. the roots stick between its teeth. the JERSEY DEVIL pulls the roots out and tosses them at the women. stone virgins stare at the falling wood. they open their mouths with their fingers and fall flat on their bellies. they pull the roots apart and wrap wood fibers around their tongues, snapping the stone and vomiting gravel. the skeletal pumpkin cries. [it isn't fair, it shouts. i am a good pumpkin and i deserve some stony meat.] one by one, the stone virgins look up. they gnash their diamond molars and tiny carat pieces fall onto the dirt. the devil tree sighs. it rattles its limbs. [just force a noose around their necks so they can swing, the devil tree says.] stone virgins crawl across the field. they move past the skeletal pumpkin and JERSEY DEVIL. they do not look at the devil tree. they lift their heads straight up in the air and breathe loudly. they snort. their chests rock back and forth, then explode. gravel covers everything. [bloodless, the stone virgins whisper. so much bloodless.] they nod their heads. their teeth jut out of their mica lips. the stone virgins stare at me. [you cannot eat the bloodless girl, the skeletal pumpkin screams. she is ours!] the skeletal pumpkin strains against the ground. it slips away from the JERSEY DEVIL and limps down the field, its body shaking and falling over its paltry root strands. [we have always wanted a bloodless girl for our digested collection, the stone virgins scream.] they leap at me. i run, my toes digging into the ground, my heels pushing my legs away. i run and the ground bends. i dart over long pathways through the dirt. i twist and the stone virgins stick in the trenches. the dirt opens up. i cling to the edge. stone virgins drop in.

i sit underground

for many days, watching the stone virgins labor beneath hammer hips and wrench pelvises. [i could have been eurydice if i had chosen to, i say] and lick my fingers until raw dirt comes off the tips. everything is brown down here. stone reeks of solid blood clots. i chip the blood stones and place the shards on my tongue. they do not melt. of course, they do not melt. nothing melts anymore. not when i want it to. not when i crave liquid. because i cannot have any. because the blood aches. no, i ache. i have been aching for the longest time and i wish i could have a drink of water. i watch the dirt. it rolls towards me, the waves lifting up then dropping. dirt granules touch my face. the stone virgins play with their long hair and concrete pushes free of their scalps. pebbles fall onto their shoulders and down their arms. i force the pebbles into my arms. my pores open. dust comes out. i am tired of the dust. i want to have liquids. i want to be a bathtub, languishing around my fluid center. but i run dry. and the little stone virgins mock me, digging their hard hands into the earth and scooping water out. they pour the moisture over their faces until droplets roll down their cheeks and burn. [we are drowning, the stone virgins cry. we are dying in the most terrible way. but that is fine. can you feel us churning? our legs are individual waves.] the stone virgins smirk and their eyes narrow. [do you want us to try tapping you for water, the stone virgins ask.] they raise their chisels. i knock them away. the stone virgins fall onto the floor. they land on their backs and moan. their stomachs thicken with endometrial fluid. uterine tissue grows on their backs and creates a mushroom cap illusion on their craniums. [we've gone infertile, the stone virgins scream. do you see?

we have nothing. our fallopian monsters have turned to force feed.] the stone virgins fling themselves onto their stomachs and beat the dirt floor until the dust crumbles. large clots cling to their tongues. i lift the stone virgins up by the backs of their necks. i shake them several times. their eyes burn. their neck meat tears. i bite their chins. i yank the meat up and over my head. i breathe the stone virgins. their stomachs stink of reeking air and i crumble their fingers until dusty. [such sorry little girls, the stone virgins say. did you see how they acted when you tore their skin up?] they shake their heads. i tear their hammers out of their hands and direct the pointed back end at their heads. i hammer and stone snaps around the hammer points. stone virgins reach around their backs. rocky fingers press against my hips. they poke my skin. water drains out of their fingers. it floods the floor and leaks up to my knees. i release them. stone virgins fall forward. they strike the ground and sink beneath the water. bubbles float to the surface and pop. the stone virgins sigh. their bodies sink to the dirt bottom. their fingers push into the stone and scratch the bedrock. i climb on their backs. i reach for the stone ceiling. my fingers catch a ledge of limestone. bony digits wrap around the stone protrusion. i put pressure on my arm muscles. i pull myself. the skeletal pumpkin leans down. [did you bury yourself, it asks and belches until a stone virgin drops out of its mouth.] the stone virgin falls past me. i climb onto solid ground.

i am a

failure of a bloodless girl. i bite my dull wrists and dust comes out. then i bite them again and nothing comes out but some gray air. but nothing liquid. because i am stone. i am a solid body and i am a failure made of bloodless mass and no fertile length of skin. i have a skeletal pumpkin and a devil tree but they make me sick. i look at their lengths of gourd flesh, trunk flesh, and twined roots, and i hate them so much my tongue nearly salivates with rage. but dust comes out. i would tear my limbs off for some saliva. i sit in a locked room covered with yellow plumage and sheets. the color warps. it turns red. it develops a bright orange hue. yellow snakes around me and i hiss until my bones break. i hiss until my mouth breaks. then i cry harder because i keep yellow stored beneath my tongue where i house a variety of dead bones in different yellow stages. of course there are stages. there is the brilliant yellow stage, when the bone is breaking. the lemon yellow stage marks a vicious red menstrual stage. the paler yellow, the mauled yellow, is the jaundice stage. and so on. and so on. until the yellow darkens. and the body decomposes. so many bodies decompose when i near them and i wrap each mangled face in yellow until sheets rot from bodily fluids. but if i die, no, when i die, can i get the yellow treatment? or is there some brown ritual i don't know about, maybe something made out of pink and left to dry in the paltry sunlight during a thunderstorm? do i drown? get bled out? lose all my dust to the rocks growing in my bones like cysts? the road refuses to lead me to the slaughterhouse. my blood tin lies unclaimed. so i am a failure. and the longer i keep my hands in my chest to draw the dust out of my fingertips, the harder it is to remove the bones. in that bony mass of calcium deposits pulled from rib cages lined with aluminum sheets, the skeletal pumpkin bleats like a sheep and lies on the floor, gourd shell flattened and heavy. [hungry, the skeletal pumpkin says. so hungry. and i need meat.] it opens its mouth to show the length of its throat and i vomit orange dust. the dust comes out in clots. the dust comes out in a thick pile topped with a hideous face of three conjoined mouths and no eyes. not even a nasal passageway or jawline. i do not deserve a full face. i get scraps, sad little pieces pulled from a mirror-lined hallway of remnants. heavy wrists adorned with sparkling gems pull free of the walls to touch me. they play with my hair. they rub the sides of my face. i bleed dust. i bleed and the fingers poke my cheeks until i bruise. dust bruises. powder cuts. i bite my fin-gernails and the jeweled wrists roll in circles until the flesh pulls free of the bones. [take a bite, the wrists whisper. take a little nibble, if you'd like. we promise the flesh will be delicious.] so i bite. because the mirrors urge me to. and because the wrist is so heavy with meat. because my stomach is empty with so many days of broken stone virgins and dead nuns creeping out of concrete crypts. so i thump the ground and bleed the meat onto the dirt. and i eat. i tear meat from muscle and muscle from bone and bone from skin and then i sit on the floor and rest from acrid digestive endeavors. while crying dust storms. while peeling loose meat off my chin. while whispering for an evil queen in the forest to leave me alone when i enter the slaughter place.

but i cannot

make sense of a constant dark that births pig-headed mushroom scraps with pieced leather skin and gelatinous bones. that darkness, stuck to the devil tree's rooted field, warped with shadows alternating between black and charcoal, silver and jet, clouds my face like nocturnal mist. i raise my hands but cannot see past the connected digits. those pig monsters gnaw my wrist and i watch dusty skin fall apart while i pick human-headed stones off the dirt ground. [we know you hunger for a slaughter place made of congealed fat, the pig-headed fungus whispers] and stacks mold spores in a pile on its head. the pig-headed mushrooms yank razor blades out of their tongues. they line the floor with sharpened silver cuts and wait for me to step. i tiptoe around the shards, my skin taut and bones guarded while the razor blades nick my ankles. they draw dust. the pig-headed mushrooms shiver with mold. algae spores erupt from their snouts and fill the air like dirt. i bat the powder away. [you won't make a mold tower out of me, i say and the pig-headed fungus hisses.] [greedy, greedy, greedy, the pig-headed fungus says] and the monsters throw themselves onto their backs. they pivot their hips in a right angle and their shoulders roll. [make us into a pork roll if you choose, the pig-headed monsters say.] they open their mouths and display lines of squared yellow teeth. pointed molars grind together. the pig-headed mushroom sprouts roll their heads until their black accordion gills crumble into truffle dust. [have a taste, the pig-headed mushrooms say. just a little one. poke your tongue out and we'll sprinkle a bit of our flesh on the tip. you'll like it. it tastes like air. but with a mustier undertone. we promise. it will make your tongue twitch with flavored joy.] thick hoofs grind together, flaking until dust falls to the ground. the pig-headed mushrooms shiver. [happy pieces of fat skin, the pig-headed mushrooms say.] i press my hands against my stomach. my fingers reach beneath my breast bones and lift the tiny bone fruit shard shaped like a knife. i twist the knife around so it rests flat against my palm. my tongue pushes out of my lips and upturns slightly to receive the fungal shavings. pig-headed monsters snort. their tiny eyes dart around their skulls. they rake abrasive stones over their cheeks and direct the pow-der flow at me. i jam the bone knife into their meat. the porcine fungus screams. [not right, they cry. not right!] their hoofs grab at the knife but slip on the calcified resin. i pull the knife out of their fat skin and jam it in again. i drag the knife down, follow-ing their bone structure. i slice thick cuts of meat off their skel-etal frames. mushroom-tainted bacon falls to the floor, followed by several fatty chops and several dozen loins. the pig-headed mushrooms nod their bulbous heads until the mushroom gills flap back and forth. they make a hammering sound. a dirt smell rises in the air. it fills my nostrils. i gag slightly. i touch my chest and an obese pressure pushes against my hands. the pig-headed mushrooms drop onto their sides. they wheeze loudly. their rib muscles drip dry. i gather the meat in a pile. raw flesh slides over my hands. it leaves wet stains in the gravely earth. [come and eat, i say.] the JERSEY DEVIL steps out of a reddish fog gathering behind my hips. the beast opens its mouth and roars loudly. [i am so hungry, it whispers.] it shoves its goat face into the meat pile and gathers the meat inside its cheeks. i pat its sides. its belly bloats with meat. the JERSEY DEVIL eats and swells.

between the skeletal
pumpkin and devil tree, the JERSEY DEVIL's stitched stomach groans with bowel pressure buildup. [is it dying, the skeletal pumpkin asks.] [can we skewer its meat, the devil tree asks.] [are you giving birth, i ask.] we press our limbs against the fleshy sides and push down. brick-like limbs push up against us. [what is happening, the skeletal pumpkin asks. i do not like the sound the monster's breathing makes.] the skeletal pumpkin rolls dirt into thick balls and plugs them into its orifices to block out the respiratory sounds. hammers bang against the JERSEY DEVIL's interior muscle. i dig my fingers into the stitches and pluck, breaking the threads but being careful not to cut the actual flesh. [huh huh huh huh huuuh, the JERSEY DEVIL pants] and hangs its stone head. the devil tree moves around the JERSEY DEVIL's backside. it touches the swollen stone and nods its branches understandingly. [i see, the devil tree says. it is going to the bathroom.] the skeletal pumpkin looks up. its shell molds around its eyes. the skeletal pumpkin scratches the green residue away. little flaking parts drop onto the outside of its mouth. [how can it have a digestive movement if it doesn't have a stomach, the skeletal pumpkin asks.] [of course it has a stomach, i say. i stitched the meat back together.] the skeletal pumpkin shrugs. it flings itself onto its back and lies flat on the ground, staring at the vaulted sky. [i do not like that creature anyway. i hope for intestinal complications, the skeletal gourd says.] i smack its shell. the skeletal pumpkin sits up. [you're being cruel. i'm ashamed by your behavior, i say.] the pumpkin pouts. it digs in the ground. i walk around the JERSEY DEVIL and tap its sides with my fingernails until i hear the hollow knock back. [you have to push, i say.] the JERSEY DEVIL lifts

its head and slams its chin against the ground. [so much pain, the JERSEY DEVIL yelps.] its backside stretches. red flesh drips out of the opening. mucoidal strings drip and pull. i gag. the fleshy fluid touches my fingertips. my skin burns. i pull my hand back. [it hurts, the stony goat cries.] the JERSEY DEVIL flaps its wings. it rises into the air. its back tightens and squeezes. bricks drop out. [what is happening, the skeletal pumpkin screams.] the bricks stack together. they create a circle. clear mucus acts like mortar. the bricks rise into the air. they leave space for a doorway, for several square windows. the JERSEY DEVIL flaps its wings harder. it claws the air. the tower stacks behind it, dropping out of the flesh. the JERSEY DEVIL strains with the stones. it pushes hard and its back legs force the bricks down. the tower stretches. [it is a subversive building, the JERSEY DEVIL cries.] it shakes its hips and breaks the final stream of stones dropping out of its body. the tower shimmers. [so much devilish behavior, the devil tree cries.] [i am outnumbered by all things named devil, the skeletal pumpkin screams.] we stare at the tower. it stands beneath the JERSEY DEVIL, tall and straight, stones shimmering with new birth. [what do we do with it, the skeletal pumpkin asks.] i touch the stone. a thin liquid burns my hands. [we dance around it, i say.] i link hands with the skeletal pumpkin and the devil tree. we move in a circle around the DEVIL'S TOWER. [fa la la la la, we sing.]

we run around
the devil's tower while the JERSEY DEVIL flips its wings into
its stitched stomach and grumbles with afterbirth labor. [get this
pumpkin-shaped flesh out of my innards, the JERSEY DEVIL
screams] and beats its head against a rock formation resembling an engorged genital. the devil's tower thins and stretches
skyward. it leaks rotten fluid onto the ground. brown water
runs through the dirt. it smells like a slaughterhouse. moisture
runs out of the tower and towards our feet, then circles backwards, re-entering the tower walls. thick concrete foundations
weaken against their masonry will. white plaster crumbles. dust
drifts to the dirt floor. the skeletal pumpkin releases its hold
on my hands. it snaps a devil tree branch and tosses the wood
on the ground. [hallowed be my pulverized shells, the skeletal
pumpkin screams] and leaps at the devil's tower. its hard shell
strikes the brick and falls apart. wet seed and stony peel land
on the floor. moisture leaches out of the hard parts and drains
into the ground. the devil tree lifts its limbs but the fluid drains
too quickly. skeletal pumpkin moisture touches the devil tree
and absorbs into the roots. skeletal pumpkin pulp flows into
the devil's tower. it puddles around the entrance, then slips
through the barred gate. orange seeds thrash. but i feel sick
of devil trees and skeletal pumpkins, whining and vomiting
red-purple pulp. i am sick of the road that doesn't reach the
slaughterhouse, no matter who walks with me. and i am sick
of being dusty. i miss my mother worm and my brothers and
sisters, even though they did not look like me. [what did you
do, i ask] and the skeletal pumpkin opens its mouth. [a curse,
it grunts] and its meat turns pale pink-yellow. its eyes close. the
devil tree lifts its limbs. it plucks at the ground. fluid spurts

out of its root tips and sprinkles the tower. bricks melt. stones warp. the JERSEY DEVIL stretches its spines and whips the air several times until it breaks the top tower. i hold my hands over my head and block the stones from my face. the devil tree falls over. its trunk snaps into thirds. branches drop off the main wood body and smash. wood pulp flies through the air. the devil tree belches skeletal pumpkin pulp. [the meat, the JERSEY DEVIL screams. that horrible meat.] its wings wrap around its head and hold its body in a vise grip. the JERSEY DEVIL falls. the devil tree bubbles and pulps. wood meat drips down its bark. i push past the devil tree parts to reach the gate. the skeletal pumpkin slides. [don't leave, the skeletal pumpkin begs] its mouth stretching into a mushroom shape. tiny green tendrils push out of its pulp. a stinking scent drips off. i gag. i kick the skeletal pumpkin's meat away. i jump over the foaming skin and fall against the metal bars. i slip down the steel. the skeletal pumpkin reaches for me. [hide in my bowels, the JERSEY DEVIL chirps.] its wings unfurl from its body and it flies into the burned trees beyond the tower. i push through the metal gates and fall onto the stone walkway. the devil tree howls. the skeletal pumpkin whines. their voices mingle and come apart. stone walls shake around me. i turn onto my stomach and crawl across the floor. damp stone cools my torso. i slide across the ground. the stone expands. it travels in thirteen separate directions. i breathe the musk in. mushrooms sprout in the stone grout. i run my fingers in the moldy meat and scoop it up. i pile the flesh onto the ground and push the tip down. i rest on my side and stare at the arched stones. mildew fluid drips from the ceiling. its puddle forms a man's face.

i plunge my
hands into the stone puddles and dig up a boy made of glass.
the stone comes away from his body slowly, limestone sliding
off his cheeks and dissolving near his hips. his mouth opens
and closes like a fish. his eyes stay shut but the lids are so translucent, i can see his pupils rolling around beneath the flesh. i
crack the stone with my fists and pry the tiles up. outside the
JERSEY DEVIL howls its stomach troubles. it shakes trees.
remnants of skeletal pumpkin meat hang near the devil's tower
gate. the flesh lingers around the metal base but does not slide
across the stone floor towards me. it quivers slightly, gelatinous body catching the pale sunlight and reflecting it back. i
turn away from the skeletal pumpkin meat and focus on the
glass boy. his lips press together and pucker slightly, drawing
his cheekbones forward. i touch his gray cheeks and my fingers
slip easily across his flesh. he is glassier than a mirror. i dig
around his sides and break the stones into pebbles. i throw the
stony pieces over my head. his fingers appear, one digit by one
knuckle, until his entire hand is exposed. his hands are larger
than mine. his veins are more pronounced. i lift his hands to
my chest and feel his heartbeat through his arteries. the glass
boy sighs softly. his chest rises. i drop his hands and pull the
stone away from his legs. his lower body comes free faster.
the stones flake away in large segments and the dirt holding
them together crumbles. slowly, his knuckles bleed. i watch a
red droplet appear beneath his glass skin. it rises up, pushing
through the surface. the bubble reaches the top of the boy's
flesh and lingers on the knuckle apex for several moments before sliding off. the blood bubble shimmers as it drags across
the skin and plops onto the stone floor. the bubble pops and

fluid spills across the floor. i pull the boy's wrists and force him into an upright position. his splintered parts bite through my arms. i touch the hanging ligaments and dust spills out of my bones. it dusts over the floor blood. the boy opens his eyes. golden irises focus on me. i let him go and the boy drops back slightly. his back tenses before he hits the ground and he holds himself in mid-air, his flesh straining. the boy sits up on his own. he holds his hands in front of his face and twists them to look at the palms and the backs. his wrists pulse. [are you my mother, the boy asks.] i shake my head. [no. i have no womb, i say.] the boy nods. he stiffens his legs, then relaxes. his toes point. the boy stretches again, then bends his knees. he stands slowly. i reach out to grab him but the boy stands and holds the pose. he steps forward. i press my lips together. the boy steps again. he reaches out. his fingers brush over my arms. he touches again and his fingers dig into my skin. the boy's fingertips touch my face. i shiver. his skin is cold. it feels moist. i hold my breath. the boy places his hand beneath my chin. he presses his wrist against my throat and holds for a moment, testing my heartbeat before releasing. his hands drop against my breasts. the boy narrows his eyes. he touches my breasts. his fingers press against the fat. [are you dusty inside, he asks.] i nod. the boy leans forward. his lips brush against mine. he stinks of sulfur. he smells like a blood bath.

the glass boy
and i hold hands in the dark. we follow steps curving to the devil's tower top and our feet strike solid stone then echo downward. the sounds spiral until they hit the ground and collapse in a melted puddle. the boy looks straight ahead, his glass cheeks reflecting the walls and part of my face. he keeps his hand on mine, squeezing gently every few minutes, and i hold my breath. i do not want him to let go of me. i like how his hands feel. i like seeing someone who is not a skeletal pumpkin or a devil tree, although i miss them and their lacquered gray frames. but i do not look back for them because they are gone and i would have to bleed all the dust out of my body to bring them back. the glass boy pauses on a short landing. he cocks his head and stares at the next flight of spiral stairs. mildew grows on the stone walls, mossy green clinging to the slick rocks, and the glass boy touches a finger to the film. he collects the moisture on his skin. he looks up but we are surrounded by stone that looks the same, hundreds of tons of heavy rock stacked together and saturated by the JERSEY DEVIL's anatomical moisture. the glass boy turns his head and looks at me. [what is it, i ask] and he reaches into his mouth to grab his tongue. his glass nails bite through the tongue and draw glassy blood droplets that shimmer on his flesh, then roll down his chin. they solidify halfway down his skin and the glass boy flicks the beads away. i catch one. it rests lightly on my palm. i curl my fingers around it and the glass breaks my skin. dust flows out of me. i shake my hand, releasing the blood droplet and sweeping the dust away. the glass boy uncurls my fingers. he prods the small cut with his fingertips. dust smears on his hands. the glass boy puts his hands to his mouth and licks the dust off.

[why do you taste like sugar, he asks.] i shake my head. the glass boy lifts my hand and puts it to his mouth. his lips press against the wound. gently he forces his tongue against the cut and laps the dust out. i close my eyes. dust drains out of my arms and legs. my stomach empties of dust. my head, my chest, my genitals, all free of dust. the glass boy brings his head away and stares at me. the dust grows again. it fills my chest and spreads upward. it drops downward. it covers every limb and bloats every organ. i am a dust mass again. shuddering slightly, the glass boy slides his sharp hands up my arms and swirls his fingers beneath my dress collar. he tugs down, exposing the base of my neck, my pronounced clavicle. glass fingers press against the bone. my fingers tap against my lips nervously, tap, tap, tap, until the glass boy touches the digits and pulls them down. he holds them tightly, so tightly my bones crunch together. i inhale and the glass boy loosens his grip. he blinks repeatedly, his eyes catching the pale evening light coming through cracks in the walls. he shimmers. [you uncovered me, the glass boy says.] i nod. [but you are not my mother, the glass boy says.] i nod again. the glass boy holds my fingers to his mouth. i close my eyes. he will bite me if i watch. he will dig his teeth shards into my skin and shred my arms of the skin. he will... he will... he will eat me alive. [marry me, the glass boy says.] the JERSEY DEVIL howls its approval.

we walk up

one thousand molding steps to the top of the tower spire. the JERSEY DEVIL trumpets loudly. [i proclaim good news tonight. the bloodless girl and glass boy will be wed before the stroke of midnight, the JERSEY DEVIL cries.] it flicks its tail and purple fire illuminates the dusky sky. i hold my hand above my eyes to block the light out. the glass boy ripples with brilliant colors. he shimmers with cut glass inside his ribs. [will you marry me, the glass boy asks.] [will you help me get to the slaughter place, i ask.] we stare at one another. [i will, the glass boy whispers.] [then i will, i say.] the glass boy licks my hands until dust pushes up from my pores and decorates his mouth with a charcoal smear. his tongue foams. white fluid dribbles down his face and plops on the floor. the glass boy leans to one side. he vomits a pale white paper scrap. the paper falls into a pile of polished red stones. i reach into the pile and unfold the page. [[[star... see the... star it is... shining this star... it is holding the... universe up it draws... the dead men forward with myrrh... in hand to the needle bed and... they find the proselytes beside the... doll they tell stories of the star and... pyrolatry the golden statues here... in the mountain peaks and nothings the... dead men remember wailing walls... and praying castles contained... in vestal virgins' dreams... the doll has no... light but is born... to prayers... to the... star.]]] he plays with his hips, his fingers tapping frantically. long parchment sheets roll out of his fingertips. marriage scrolls. i lift each sheet to my tongue and wait patiently for the paper to melt to a thick white cake on my tongue surface. the glass boy lifts a loose stone from a turret and heaves it against his breast. his bones shatter. the glass boy lies on his side and plays with the rock mounds scattered across the tower top. i rest beside him and place my head on his shoulder. my lungs move with his. he spews paper and i spew dust. [we are wed, the glass boy says.] [we are wed, i say.] the glass boy tilts his hips to the right and glass crystals drop out of the space. i touch the crystals. they collect beneath my fingernails and shimmer brilliantly. i squint my eyes. my skin blisters from the light. the glass boy places my fingers in his mouth and bites the crystals out. [you cannot have the glass, he says] and swallows, tearing his throat up from the inside. glass blood wells up. he swallows the internal blood and his stomach bloats with ingested fluid. the woods scratch the air. flutes force their ways through the branches. i look up. the JERSEY DEVIL curls in a ball in the hollow of a dead tree and sleeps. its scaled hide pales to a medium gray shade. i can barely see him in the dropping night. [do you hear something, i ask.] the glass boy rises at the waist. he follows my gaze. [is it steak, he asks.] i shake my head. [no, i whisper. something else. a hungry thing. i think.] the glass boy crawls to the stone edges and looks down. he leans back and stares at me. i look into the dark horizon. sinew-like clouds wind around the air and constrict water flesh. they reach for my throat. [there is nothing there, the glass boy says. only red eyes. but they have glowed since the tower's beginning. and ours.] i look over the side. my hair falls in my face. red eyes blink. and blink. and blink.

mother worm you
breathe with me and i season you with salt. i imagine you are
here in the devil's tower with me, mother worm. i even see you
writhing on your hook and i worry about my marriage. a glass
boy heavy with crystalline fragments fastens his teeth in my
skin and tears until i bleed dust over everything. but you writhe,
like the little worm you have tried being since birth. i worry for
you, mother worm. i worry that your skin sloughs off at night
when i should be feeding you sour milk tinged with yellow food
dye. i worry that your stomach does not process meat willingly.
i worry and i worry and then i cut one of your thirteen faces
off to hang in the sky. the constellation worm. the mother
star. mother worm in all her segmented glory. while your children sit on the ground, coping with their years of ground dust.
maybe you were beautiful in a past life and looked something
like the intestines tucked into the JERSEY DEVIL's digestive
tract. but maybe you were something else, some expanse of
skin spread flat across a broken window in some abandoned
steel mill desperate to churn coal smoke again. mother, may i
have some of your skin? may i? if i ask nicely, can i commit
maternal cannibalism and resolve to talk about the act with
splintered wood walls trying to crack their nails? the glass boy,
now my glass husband, now the glassy spouse, plays with my
dust while i bathe in dirt. he drops the dust from one hand
to the other, sprinkling it around and i do not like the way
his skin looks when glowing with such purpose. [stop being a
husband figure, i say] and the glass boy just smiles. he does not
know how to stop being a husband and start being a hunter.
mother worm, what shall we hunt today? an alleyway of houses marked with white windows? thumping roadways bumpy

with decomposing bodies? or mouths split in half and torn upwards? what do you prefer? or should we hunt the mother worm, just hang her on a meat hook by her tail end and let her kill herself? should we hunt you? you might taste bitter, like fresh parsley. or you might have a meatier flavor similar to aged beef. i cannot tell. and if i am to know for certain, i will have to bite your stomach for a taste. mother worm, i have done terrible things. i have eaten precious pink eye orbs and brutally mauled BABA women and left skeletal gourds to die while i traversed the length of a thin tower stretching into a bloody sky. and i have pulled my fingers until the bones snapped, then thrown the pieces at a red-eyed creature far away from me. i am not a hunter, mother worm. i am a bloodless girl being hunted by a thing with red eyes. it follows me wherever i go and gnashes its teeth while i sleep. a little boy ate his sister in front of me. decide what meaning seems right with you. only know it ended with the girl's crying. and maybe something else, but i can't know for certain because i couldn't watch thighs combing the wreckage around an oven base. i dug my nails in, too. and i lifted sinew and charcoal to my face. mother worm, i hold the glass man between my thumbs and he pushes a splinter into my skin, then bites my flesh until dust comes out. he drinks, pulling the glass shard while chewing. his stomach burns. i give him steaks but he vomits. i feed him vegetables and he defecates. it is the same with air, fluid, wood, and metal. my glass husband is hungry, mother worm. i don't know what to feed him.

red eyes follow
a length of beating road that wheezes when i walk. [there must
be steak somewhere, the glass boy says.] he tenses his throat
and yanks his tongue repeatedly. glass breaks in his hands and
he throws his meat to the ground. [i want a child, the glass boy
says. have my child.] he opens his mouth and moves his tonsils
around. white foam drips off his cheek bones. the gelatinous
fluid sinks into my hands. i gag. the fluid puddles in my hands.
i wipe it away. [i can't have children, i say. i'm barren. my womb
won't work. that's why i didn't birth you.] the glass boy smiles.
he spreads his lips until they are clear. his crystal structure
angles towards the light and reflects the white back. my eyes
ache. i touch the edges and they tear. i squeeze my eyes shut. [i
don't want children, i say.] the glass boy narrows his eyes and
beats his fists against his chest. internal organs shatter. glass
falls from his ribs into his stomach pit. he turns to one side
and vomits violently, his mouth stretching to release piles of
glass shards stained in one thousand red shades. [i won't have
your children, i say. do not ask me for them again.] i press my
hands against my dusty stomach and gasp loudly. behind the
glass boy, the red eyes blink again. they crush together and ruin
several large trees. the glass boy gathers my hair in his hands.
he pulls until my scalp tears. i touch my head. dust comes out
of my hair. pinkish dust rises out of the red eyes. i swat the
fog away. red eyes grow in the dark. red eyes rise out of the
dirt. red eyes and red eyes and red eyes until the eyes are so
red, they are almost white and i go blind from staring too long.
the glass boy shakes my arms. i reach out and touch the red
eyes. red gelatin clings to my fingers. i shake it free but the red
eyes shimmer and hold tightly to my dusty skin. [eat the red

eyes, the glass boy says] and sinks his teeth into the red parts. he bites several times and brings his mouth back. fur covers his mouth. the glass boy picks the hairs off and tosses them to the floor. red eyes squeak. red eyes flutter. red eyes turn in circles. they turn on themselves and behind the red eyes is a furry moth body that beats its wings while twisting its furred antennae tight around the base. the glass boy leaps at the moth body. he wraps his legs around the moth torso and tightens his thighs. [never let me go, he cries] and digs his front teeth into the moth body. the moth body lifts its arms. it pokes the glass boy's shoulders. i watch closely. my fingers itch. i look at the palms, and tufts of gray hair poke out of my skin. i dig my fingernails into the hair mass and yank the strands out individually until the skin puckers. the glass boy hisses. [what are you doing to yourself, the glass boy asks.] he drops off the moth body and wraps his arms around my throat. i push him away. i throw the glass boy on the ground. the moth body leans at the waist and vomits rocks over the glass boy until his glass frame shatters. the moth body bleeds thickly from many fresh wounds covering the flesh beneath the fur coat. [what do you want, i ask.] [to love you, the glass boy shouts. and to have a child with you.] [light, the moth body whispers.] it drops its head slightly. i step over the glass boy. his fingers dig into my feet. i kick him away. i step towards the moth body. gently i place a hand on its insect torso. i feel for a light bulb within the fur.

but i only

want the glass boy's vertebrae. [i don't want children, i say.] i skewer him on a stick and pull his flesh off the bone until his muscles ache. [are you sick, the glass boy asks. you are my wife and should be kinder to my skin.] [i warned you, i say.] the glass boy lies on a metal table. he mauls the sides of his face and yanks his skin downward to the bottoms of his jaws. the glass boy shatters slightly. his glass trembles. i push a pair of scissors into his skin and tear the muscle into pieces. the glass boy bleeds thick viscous fluids. yellow mucus drips off his wrists. i bite the glass boy with some broken stones and push the rocks down my throat. they fill my stomach. the dust settles around my abdomen. my skin floods. [i have no skin, the glass boy screams.] but he has skin. he has so much skin that it piles around his bones and crumbles to the floor. i stomp on his skin. i rip his skin until it sours. i throw it into a vat of metal and wait for it to boil to a thick gelatin. i have no skin. i have no more skin at all. i scrape my bones and the glass boy crumbles. he falls to the floor. i saw through his bones. the red eyes tear through my stomach and throw acidic dust onto the floor. the dust burns through boards made of compressed bones and rusted sinew. i look down the hole and stare at the steaming flesh beneath. [is this something discarded or a piece of skin yanked off a pair of bones, i ask.] the red eyes twitch. moth wings flutter behind the red eyes and smash into miles of plaster walls. the glass boy twists into a circle. his backbone rises up and leaves red marks across a pair of seared steaks. i push my fingers into the bones and lift them up. his skin rips. i peer beneath the flesh and see little green eyes poking out of his flesh. the glass boy pushes his fingers into the meat. the eyes squish around his fingertips. i flake the flesh away and tear the spinal cord out. the glass boy hisses. he pushes his mouth out and drills his tongue into the floor. the glass boy falls over. his skin goes slack. i tear his hands off his arms and throw them at the red eyes. the moth body opens around its middle. the meat slides through the gap and dissolves in the moth body. [hungry, the moth body sighs] and pulls its skin folds together. i sit on the floor. the spineless glass boy flops on the floor. he stabs his head on a wooden railing and sinks to the floor. i step on his chest. [my wife, the glass boy whispers. my wife. i love you.] the glass boy lifts his fingers slightly and drops them onto my hands. i pull back. i lift his flesh up and it puddles on the floor. i wind his vertebrae around my throat. i pull it tight until my neck narrows. i stand up. the red eyes follow me. i stroke the spinal cord gently. [but i love you, the vertebrae whisper. i love you, i love you. where did the red eyes go?] the vertebrae shudder. i stare through the bones. the glass boy's face pushes up from the separate bones. his many faces cling to the nervous cord and open. their tongues shiver and drip saliva. i dust the spinal cord with dust and tap the bones. the hollow sound vibrates through my head. the red eyes float to the floor. they puddle up. i lean over and dip my fingers into the moisture. ripples flow through the red moth eyes. [are you hungry, the glass boy nervous cord asks. you should eat something.] the glass boy bones hum. my throat is sore.

lights fall out

of my throat. bulbs and strings and tiny circles shatter on the ground. glass cuts my feet. the red eyes open and close, fanning the glass into my face. i push my fingers into the red eyes and spill steak onto the floor. there are lights here. there are lights there. red lights and blue lights and white lights and green lights and heated lights and cool lights and shattered lights and new lights. lights that pulse beneath our flesh and come out of the walls, mimicking moons and suns and stars without begging for a taste of human flesh. if i knew the meat i know now, i might not leave it to fester in the basement with the mold faces and the moth wings. [i know wings that should have been born as entire men and i know men who should have panicked at the first onslaught of moth genitals, i say.] but the red eyes don't answer. they blink and flutter. tense faces resembling the glass boy rise out of the air and settle on my skin like ticks. they bite my skin. everything bites me. these faces. pots and pans. heavy skin flecks with golden particles clenching the narrow pores. special meat. and heavy meat. and something else that could be a mother worm if it were seasoned with salt instead of pepper. but i say things that the tower does not want me to whisper and i follow roads heavy with white-washed windows and if i bite the sides of a meaty throat, then it is to say my prayers in the middle of the night instead of skewer my wrists on a butterfly pole. that butterfly pole should be a spider skewer should be a dragonfly pillar but i know sticks and only sticks. just like a wing is a wing no matter the head it stays attached to until the ax falls. and i have axes tucked into my back. i keep the blades close to the spinal cord around my neck. i hold the blades until my fingers slice in half. then i tremble and my body feels whole again. but it never feels new. that is impossible. it has no meat to feel whole with. just skin. and heavy metal deposits yanked out of my muscle and tossed with some alcohol derived from vinegar. this and that. while the moth body says its prayers on a bag of beads. as if i would take a butter knife to its thorax and split the shell into individual steaks roasted in heavy fats. but mother worm hammers inside of me. [bite it. bite it dead, she hums.] mother worm bites my stomach lining until my dust bloodies. but my dust does not bloody. it stays gray and dull, although each mouthful has a distinctive copper taste. the dust pulls my eyes deeper into my head. it wrenches the eye sockets closed so that the gelatin puckers and pushes. i cannot see through the gelatin. it smears my forehead. it singes my skin like a lamp post. because it is a lamp. and a light. and a glowing match. if i keep it illuminated, i will be able to see every night and the moth body will stain its teeth yellow to match its pneumonia lungs. furred skin has the same secrets i do. we are both hungry. sometimes, we shave the hair from our skin and panic over our nudity by filling our nasal passages with water. or we pop every red pore on our stomach with a knitting needle stolen from an asbestos-filled basement. and worse, we drop black ink into our eyes and wait impatiently for the pigment to fill our gelatin. then we have black eyes and it is better than red eyes or silver eyes. it reflects better in the light.

mother worm in

my skin bites my muscle until i am bright yellow with rot. mother worm crumbles in my lungs and my ankles twist backwards.
[why do you try to eat me, worming mother creature, i ask] and
i think i see mother worm squirm through double-doors made
of solid red glass. i follow but cannot get past the glass sheets.
i push my hands against the material and my nails scratch, but
my body does not slide through. [i must get behind, i cry] and
stroke the nervous system suspended from my neck. my glass
boy husband's spinal column twitches slightly as i scratch the
glass. [it hurts me, i say.] the glass boy nervous system bites the
sides of my neck leaving pale gray marks over my skin. i pinch
each wound center and it bursts. blood dust smears my fingertips. i cry and my eyes water with pain. [i could have kept you
from feeling anything, the glass boy spinal cord whispers.] the
many glass boy vertebral faces pucker their lips and blow kisses
in my direction. i swat the affection away and focus on my
maternal worm squirming down a dusty hallway, her tail swelling from the presence of rock salt. she quivers upon reaching
every corner and i watch the mother worm for an hour before
rattling the doors so loudly, they break down the center. i fit
through the crack and enter the new hallway. light bounces past
my head. it illuminates the far wall and i stare through a reddish fog as mother worm zigzags down a corridor to reach the
exterior wall. [but mother, i cry. what did i do wrong?] the gray
hallway darkens. i cannot see anything, just some flesh dangling
in front of my face, and too many glass boy faces pricking my
skin with their front teeth. [should spinal cords have teeth, i
ask] and the glass boy faces narrow their eyes. they flop to one
side and bite my shoulder blades hard. i dig my nails into the

spinal cord and rupture three bones. mucus spills out of the bone mouths. it wets the floor behind me. i move on, my eyes dusting over from so much dryness in the hallway. [mother worm, i call and knock on the walls.] paint flakes off the surface and long sheets curl down before dropping to the floor. i kick the paint pieces away. they shatter into asbestos. white dust fills the air. i cover my mouth and nose with my hands. the glass boy vertebrae move their tongues around and whip me with the nervous centers. yellow wicks strike me until my skin bleeds from physical abuse. i twist a spinal cord end until it snaps. a single bone drops into my hand. the glass boy vertebra stares at me. it looks at its conjoined cord and screams. i drop the bone and crush it beneath my heel. glass boy dust rises a foot in the air, then rests back on the ground. it settles into the floorboards. [mother worm, i cry.] i turn left and enter a narrow walkway. a red light flashes. i peer down the walkway and see the mother worm curled up on a rusted meat hook. [what are you doing, mother worm, i ask.] she stretches her body and the center sticks to the hook. i lean closer. the meat hook edge pierces her skin and holds her in place. [mother worm, i whisper. you've been skewered.] she looks down at her center and opens her mouth slightly. reddish fluid drips out of her throat and dribbles down her body. she blinks slowly and her eyes close. i lift my mother worm off the hook. she rots away in my hand. she is not there at all.

the glass boy
spinal cord yanks me across five white-washed houses to reach
the golden altar at the end of a small cul-de-sac. [give up your
heart, the glass boy spinal cord says] and reaches for the altar.
the cord strains. its length tightens around my neck. i gag and
break the vertebral bones in my hands. [this is not the slaughter place. you said you would help me reach my blood tin, i
say.] vertebrae fall to the floor and shatter into thousands of
tiny dusty marrow beads. the altar glimmers. it is an altar in
the woods, one of many little altars dedicated to various cannibal gods and religious denizens craving blood lust and blood
flow and poor circulation. and the altar grows in length until it
covers thirteen parts of the world, then expands to fill in the
rest. [do not stop thinking in tongues, the altar says] and bites
my ankles. it is a beautiful altar with many gems formed from
human heads. they glimmer and drip beneath the streets. [give
us your heart, the altar says and beats its gold against the side-
walks]. metal echoes against the concrete. i cover my ears and
my eyes bulge out of my skull. i see through the altar to the
meat stacked up on the other side and all that meat is frozen
with rotten worms. [mother worm, i whisper] and fling myself
at the muscle. i pull the fat to one side. i twist the fat around
my fingers and increase my dust blood tenfold. the mother
worm squirms around a meat stack. she opens her mouth and
swallows fatty beef without chewing. her jaws stretch and she
is like a snake. [mother worm, i cry. i've been looking for you.
my husband has been bad to me. he strangles me when i think
of bright blue things.] mother worm drops off the meat stacks
and darts towards the white-window houses lining the block.
[mother worm, i scream] and chase her squirming figure. [i

have salt for you!] but mother figure does not look back. the golden altar pulls its legs out of the ground. it stretches its golden spine and reaches into the air. [i still demand your heart. it has more dust than a kidney stone. come here. i want to eat, the golden altar screams and bangs its body against the ground.] the sidewalks break into sections. mother worm squirms across a large lawn and pushes her body through a large wooden door. the frame slams behind her. the golden altar lifts the flesh near its feet. i sprint across the grass and fling myself at the door. i break the wood down. the white windows open and close. they blink like eyes. [who said you could come inside, they ask.] they hammer their nails against the floor. [did we, they ask. did you? did they? do those stairs think they can betray us?] the windows slam again and i see mother worm squirm up a flight of rotten stairs. i cling to the railing and follow. she drops into the spaces in the steps. she wiggles her body up and down, until the meat stops and her face stretches to one thousand times its original size. the golden altar slams its body against the house's exterior. it bites the white-washed windows and pulls the many wooden blinds down. [you cannot strip the house naked, the white windows shout.] they sink their rusted nails into the golden altar and pull its lacquer off its wood. i reach the next floor. mother worm rushes into the first room and slams the door. i grab the heated knob and turn. it opens. i face a room filled with liquid water and heaving waves of bloody fat rush for my mouth.

rancid meat in

a closet filled with mother worms saturates my feet. [this is not the moisture i have been craving for at least fifteen hundred years, i shout] and the mother worms cringe in the plaster. my mother worm departs from her maternal cohorts to wind her squirming body around my ankles. [mother, please, i whisper. i shouldn't be punished for the salt crimes.] the mother worm whispers softly. sound comes off her segments and tears at my knees. meat drops off my bones and fills her tiny sucker mouth. i kick the mother worm away. [why are you eating me? i'm not food, i cry.] downstairs the golden altar pushes its wooden frame through the doorway. it breaks the walls. golden bones fall out of its bowels and drop through the floors. the bones land in a dusty basement that i can smell with my hands. the mother worm wraps around my fingers and tightens on the bones until they snap in half. [don't be scared, the walls shout. you need some skin in your life.] they press together and i fall through the floor. the mother worm follows me down the hole. we drop onto the bones and roll down the sides. the bones fall onto my head. the golden altar looks over the edge of the hole and grunts. [my meat has fallen, the golden altar whispers.] it stretches down and its wood swats at my head. [does the meat rot, the white-washed windows ask. does the meat feel wrong? would it be slimy? or would it be soft? should we love the hungry meat or should we bite the windowpanes?] they slam closed again and the golden altar circles the hole. i crawl through the broken bones. the mother worm forces her way through a hollow femur and digs the marrow out. fat drips down her face. the mother worm whips her tongue around her head and bites a wall in half. plaster hangs out of her mouth.

the mother worm sighs. her chest heaves. i throw the bones at her. the mother worm slips into the concrete floor and tosses rocks at me. [does the bloodless girl fall apart when the golden altar touches her skin, the white windows ask. does she try to eat the satan meat without chewing? oh, do we feel anything for that child and her dusty innards?] the white windows slam against the walls and bite. their plaster tears apart. i push bones into my mouth. dry enamel crumbles on my tongue. my stomach swells with resin and lacquer. the mother worm twists into a hole and blocks the entrance with her gut. [salt, the white windows ask. salt? what to do with salt? do we bite the salt? do we eat the salt? do we sleep with the salt? salt? can we have pepper instead? can we at least have some rocks?] white windows rise up and slam down. white windows push out of the walls and drop onto the living room floor. glass shatters. i push my fingers into the hole and scoop the mother worm out. she bites my hand. dust pours out of my thumb. it covers the floor. i scoop the dust back into my hands. [come here meat flank, the golden altar shrieks.] its splinters grasp my hair and yank sharply. i rise to my feet. the golden altar pulls me through the ceilings. broken wood passes me. i push splinters away. i fall into the living room. the golden altar traces the curve of my spine. [should i eat you in one bite or two, the golden altar asks.] [or three, the white windows ask.]

i fight golden

flesh and skewer the altar on a railing made of human skin. [did you think i would let you eat my digestive dust, i ask and the golden altar squeals.] it moves its splintered legs up and down, then tears its heart out. it is a pale black organ but not a gray one. mucus drips out of the many chambers. the heart squeaks as it drips. the golden altar pushes the heart at my face. i bat the fluid-filled sack away. i hate the noxious rot smell coming off its dimpled flesh. the golden altar waves the heart in the air, then stuffs it down its chin. [how do you have a heart, i ask. and how do you eat with parts that don't belong to your mouth?] the golden altar fidgets. glass boy vertebrae around my neck tighten until i cannot breathe. i gasp for air. the golden altar touches the bones. the glass boy bites the altar several times. [you aren't allowed to touch me, the glass boy says. you aren't royalty. you are just a hungry monster with too many eyes.] but the golden altar has no eyes. i stare at the wooden frame and see nothing but polished sides and too much paint. the glass boy snaps his teeth. his jaw works in circles. [i have a love-hate relationship with the floor, the glass boy mumbles] and drops off my neck. his spinal cord turns away. i watch the bones grind against the concrete and squirm away. [you look like a mother worm, i shout.] the glass boy spinal cord snakes its way towards a sewer grate. i extend my arms past the golden altar and grab the glass boy spinal cord by its tapered tail. the spinal cord shrieks. [do not touch me, it says.] i string the cord around my neck and tie the two ends together in a permanent knot. the bones click together, secur-ing the knot so that only a chisel can break the bond apart. the golden altar frowns. [i think you stink of marriage, the golden altar says.] [i do stink of marriage. that is my husband, i say.] the golden altar drops me. i fall onto the floor. the white windows, tucked into the walls far behind me, raise their voices over the windowsill. [is she having an affair if she wears her husband chain and lets the golden altar grab her skin? or is that monogamy? and what is that vinegar smell in the air, the white windows ask.] they press their sills together. the golden altar groans. [i will eat you anyway, the golden altar says. because i hate you. and i love your meat smell.] the altar center unfolds. a thick wooden tongue pushes out of the space and thrashes the air. [give me your meat, the golden altar's center shouts] and lunges forward. the glass boy spinal cord leaps in front of my face. it drags me along. the elongated spinal cord end rises in the air and smacks the golden altar's tongue away. [you cannot touch my wife, the spinal cord says. sacred vows cannot be broken. not by you and not by her machete lungs. she is my wife forever. whether she hallucinates or not. whether she wears my bones or not. whether she digests my flesh or not.] the spinal cord cuts through the jutting altar mouth and snaps the tongue into tiny worms. the segmented creatures fall to the floor. [is one of them the mother worm, i ask and the glass boy spinal cord snarls in my direction.] [stop worrying about your mother, he says. she isn't here. you seasoned her to death years ago.] the spinal cord pulls me forward. i look at the ground. there are no worm marks for me to follow.

[was there ever
a mother worm, i ask the white windows.] i sit outside a half-
broken house, the white windows clinging to a small section of
wall decorated with aluminum siding. [did you want there to be
a mother worm, the white windows ask.] [of course i did. but
she wasn't there, i say] and lean over to rest my fingers on the
dirt floor. the glass boy spinal cord strains against my neck. [i
want to travel, the glass boy bones shout. even bones get tired
of monotony. can't we go somewhere else?] the spinal cord
settles across the tops of my breasts and sighs loudly. [is there
somewhere else, the white windows ask.] tiny nail tongues pull
loose and maul the skin near my shoulder. i flick the painted
metal away. they fly past the white windows and drop onto the
hidden living room floor. [so sad, the white windows ask. or
very happy?] they shrug. their frames loosen and glass panes
pull out of the wooden sides. i stare at the abandoned street.
[what's past that hilltop across the road, i say] pointing at a
small incline in the distance. the white windows sigh. [is there
anything there, they ask. or is that just a lie?] i stand up. the
wooden porch steps creak beneath my feet. the glass boy spinal
cord lifts up again. [you keep biting me, i say] and the necklace loosens as much as the knot will allow. [the bones bite
into the tapped spinal marrow, the glass boy spinal cord says.]
[what marrow, the white windows ask. what bones? should
we know the difference between the two? or are our panes on
backwards? do panes have anything to do with brains? must
we remain so confused?] the white windows pick at their individual locks and slide their panes shut. the glass boy spinal
cord hisses. [this is nonsense, he cries. all of it. the flesh and
the hill rising in the horizon. what do we do with that? eat the

incline? hope to dig beneath the dirt and find another sexual partner?] i stroke the spinal cord gently. the bones bump along my palm. i squeeze the knotted tip and drop my hands to the floor. [i thought there might be an opening, i say. some kind of doorway that would feel good in the midnight air. couldn't you see us living a domestic life housed inside a hilltop domicile?] the glass boy spinal cord whimpers softly. [is that why you let me free in the great beyond, the glass boy spinal cord asks.] [if you mean is that why i released you from the floor, no. i only let you out because i thought you were the most beautiful man i had ever felt beneath my feet, i say.] the glass boy spinal cord hangs limply down my back. it bumps against my spine, bruising its bones and mine. i arch my back and the glass boy spinal cord falls away. [there, i say. that's better.] i point at the hilltop. it breaks through the darkness, casting shadows to its many sides. i stand and the glass boy spinal cord falls against me. it quivers slightly and wraps around my hips. [i want to see what's inside the hill, i say.] i spit up a dust clot. it smacks the floor. the white windows clamor. [what was that thing? was it dust? can we eat it? we would like to eat, wouldn't we, the white windows ask.] they strain for the dust clot. [tell me what's in the hill, i say.] i lift the dust up and hold it just beyond their panes. [do you believe in gray things, in monsters made of bronze? sour strings of dry blood, they ask.]

the spinal cord
pushes into my navel. the glass boy vertebrae vomit into my
skin. hard vomit pushes through my skin. my flesh sags and
tenses. it puckers around the spinal cord. [what are you doing
to me, i ask.] the spinal cord sharpens and drills further into my
muscle. i turn towards the white windows. they sigh. [what does
the man do to the woman, the white windows ask.] they tap and
plaster slides down their glass panes. i reach around and catch
the plaster. [do not touch anything solid when we are in the
midst of copulation, the spinal cord says.] the glass boy bones
slide up and down the cord. they leap at my face and push their
lips against mine. [fertilize, they shout. we must fertilize.] pollen pokes out of their eyes. i wipe the yellow powder away. [it
is time for the reproduction, the glass boy bones say.] [what is
reproduction, the white windows ask. the process by what does
what? or the white paint dries too slowly? or the flesh rots until muscles hang off? what is the what we should know about
when we are near the bloodless girl?] the spinal cord pushes
along. my meat sinks into my body. reddish dust wells up in
the hole. [do not bleed, the glass boy vertebrae whisper. do not
bleed because it is sad when the only wife bleeds. we only want
a child with you. we just want to bite your skin.] i scramble up
the steps to the front of the house but the spinal cord reaches
from my abdomen to my back. i pause and double over, my
hands scratching at the stiff bones until the enamel flakes off.
i sink to my knees and the spinal cord moves with me. [you
are a good girl, the glass boy spinal cord says. but we are better bones.] i gag. dusty vomit spills out of my mouth and dusts
over the floor. the white windows watch. they sag around their
centers and i wipe dust from my lips. my chest aches. i vomit

and the dust flows down the steps. dust collects in between the spinal cord bones. dust fills the marrow spaces. [should we vomit if we are ready to sire children, the white windows ask.] they shake their sills and i sit up. dust hangs onto my chin. i brush the dust away and push my fists against my stomach until the meat ruptures. my ovaries break and dusty eggs flow out. the spinal cord punctures my lungs and slips out. yellow pollen mixes with my dust clots. i gasp for air. [if you're going to run to some unknown hill, then you should take our child with you, the glass boy bones whisper.] the spinal cord tears free of my stomach and embeds its ends in the ground. i wrench the cord up, lifting several pounds of dirt with the hooked body. the spinal cord waves in the air. it flips up and its center cuts through my stomach. [somewhere past that mirror stash, should we find our menstrual cramps, the white windows ask.] they press their glass together and wait for the outer panes to shatter. [what if we cannot die by our own hammers, the white windows ask.] they fidget on the walls. i slide down the stairs and crawl towards the street. my limbs ache. the spinal cord hangs behind me. i reach the road and force my feet over the curb. the hill looms above me. my stomach jumps. i bite my thumb and draw dust. [now we know the fertility worked, the spinal cord says.] it pierces my tongue tip. my muscle clenches. dust drifts out. i crawl towards the hill. i watch the foaming top.

i bite the

dark rising out of the hilltop across the street. it is a long street
and an even larger hilltop. i walk slowly, the spinal cord winding
around my neck, gelatinous wind cutting my skin until i bleed
dust on the asphalt. if i bleed dust everywhere, then the hungry
light fixtures might not bite me. and the golden altars will pray
to their own gods instead of my innocent ankles and i might
be able to dig my way into the hill without losing my dusty
womb to the goat-headed monsters mewling on the dirt floor.
so i walk and the street turns to quicksand. it pulls me down.
it bites my hands and drags me. i fall into the street. i drift
with the liquid concrete and my dust drifts out of my body,
collecting on the street surface, marking my path. but i do not
walk straight and i did not walk straight and i will never walk
straight. the dust proves this. it follows my motions and none
of them are straight. they lean to the left then dart to the right
and alternate for a time before flowing backwards. i repeat myself several times and each time my skin feels rancid beneath
my nails. [that is the baby talking, the spinal cord whispers.
you have our child in your skin.] i pinch the spine between two
fingernails. the nervous system cuts short. it gags and its yellow
fatty parts drip away from my fingers. the marrow strikes the
floor and then the street is whole again although i stay stuck
in the middle, my eyes rolling in tight circles. i stare at the hill.
i stare at the hill for hours and the hill is the most beautiful
thing i have ever seen and i want to be in that hill and i want to
eat that hill but the street refuses to release me. so i bite. i lean
over and i bite the street. i tear the asphalt up and the glass boy
spinal cord around my neck tightens to stop me, but it cannot
seal my mouth no matter how hard it tries because my jaws do

not listen to anything but dusty food and a spinal cord is not a meal. a spinal cord was never a meal or a husband or a piece of useful skin. just a spinal cord. and me stretching my limbs until my face aches from so much effort to reach the hill on the other end. [what if the hill devours your skin, the white windows scream.] they rattle violently, glass panes shaking in the frames, each panel threatening to spill past the iron sections. i crawl across the street, my body forced down on my stomach, and digestive meat tears under my ribs. it tears until i have the same chopped liver appearance that my favorite JERSEY DEVIL had, wherever he might be now, cutting his hoofs off in the hopes he might grow feet or pulling his boulder shell off his back to let wings spread farther. the street grows around me. it darkens and tiny crystals rise out of the walkways to mock me. they shrink and glow. they open and darken. i scratch my cheeks. i scratch my face. i watch the white windows and their glass shards spread apart but reach for nothing. [are you weaker than the hilltop's anatomical denizen, the white windows sigh.] they shake their panes. i shake the road. i grip the asphalt with both hands and shake until it comes loose. [no one will ever eat me alive again, i say] and i pull myself over the curb. the hill remains above me across the sidewalk. i slide over the painted stone. i grip the grass on the other side and pull until the blades tear in my hands. i have green fingers now. i am at the hill.

i am pregnant.

but it is impossible that i am pregnant. i don't have a womb. that is inaccurate. the only womb i have is a dusty cluster of cells centered in my abdomen. it bursts three times daily, the mass rupturing around its edges just enough for the dust to leak out and run over the floor. then i feel sick. then i feel so sick i fall to one side vomiting my guts. my guts are squirming things resembling mother worms. mother worms are meant to be heard not seen, and if they keep their worm bodies stuffed in the kitchen counter, then they might be worth more. worth as much as a piece of skin plucked right off my head and thrown into an oven pretending to be a cannibal. but we're all cannibals, no matter how much meat we eat that isn't our own and if we chew the meat to the point of digestion and spit it out, does that mean we are lapsed sinners? but i am a sinner and you are a sinner and the glass boy cord around my neck is a sinner. it is the king of sinners. it is the matriarch of sinners, drenched in marrow substance and laid across a baked road-way to dry to a whispering pulp pulled out of tree scars. i have more scars than i know what to do with and the scars grow on top of one another humming until the flesh sighs its muscle release and grunting, grunting, grunting. is it another grunting day? or is it a grunting holiday i cannot sit through? i cannot sit through slaughter or meat or sinew or glass shards or religious movements or burning at the stake. i cannot touch the stake because it will make me fall asleep like that famed literary rape victim. the rape victim closed her eyes, went to sleep, and woke up one hundred years later surrounded by three-eyed children pawing at her imploded breasts. the same breasts the rapist had poked until the girl squealed. squealed like an attic roof.

like a soul pushing through an eye without touching the needle sides. but i have needles and sides stuffed with raw meat and pink flesh. i keep the raw meat tucked into my wrists. my wrists bend and that is my version of voodoo. it is dusty voodoo, of course. but voodoo impregnates me against my will and when i get pregnant, i cannot see straight. i cannot see now. i cannot see the way the walls conjoin and split apart. i cannot see how my legs split into one hundred directions that are not individual rape victims. i cannot see how the pregnancy has raped my body into a vinegar plant. because i guzzle vinegar while hungry to keep the moisture at bay. what i wouldn't give for a bay leaf stuck into the back of my throat, rough herb edges scraping my throat until i cannot squeeze a sound out. i cannot squeeze dirt out. not out of this body or the one that might come later or the one that came before. because before i was not ready for mother time. and now i am not ready for mother time. and if this mother time settles on my tongue until it grows a bright blue food fuzz, i will tear my hands off at the dirt and throw them into the hilltop pit. we all have pits. our bowels and our stomachs and our dirt. all that dirt collected in our tongues and spewing out of our eyes. and that is how it stinks. the flesh and the sinew and the rot. the dirt pregnancy growing within me. if i explode... when i explode... i will chew the glass boy spinal cord until it is limp meat. i will eat it, bones, dirt, and all.

i birth dirt.

i birth dirt. i birth dirt. i birth dirt. i birth dirt. i birth dirt. and it hurts. it hurts me and it hurts the hill who hangs between my legs and yanks at the dirt growth. dirt clusters beneath my nails. dirt acts like a tumor pushing against my hands until the muscle is so numb that i am convinced it does not hang onto me any longer. the dirt comes. the dirt pours out of the walls. the dirt comes out of plaster walls then out of my walls. the dirt bleeds out of me and the glass boy spinal cord tears at my waist, releasing the dirt clots by striking my flesh with his bony fists. [let the child out, the glass boy spinal cord cries. just let it go free. or it will kill us all.] the glass boy spinal cord reaches through the hilltop innards to get at the fresh air beyond the outer walls. the hilltop holds its breath. it pulls its walls together, trapping the spinal cord tip in a thick layer of raw bedrock. [this is not right, the glass boy spinal cord says. that is my wife. and she must give birth before i expel my lungs' contents without permission.] the glass boy spinal cord rocks back and forth. the dirt comes out in waves. blue waves pour out of my eyes. yellow waves heave in my chest. the red dirt waves come up my throat and drop out of my mouth. the dirt covers the floor. it covers me. i swat the dirt away but the dirt does not come loose. the dirt is a net, is a fabric sheet and the dirt refuses to break into particles. the clots and clumps stay close together. they form a boulder. they rake over my skin until my dust flows out. i lose dryness and dirt. i wait for the moisture to collect in my mouth but the dirt just settles in the back of my throat, scraping the flesh up until i gag. i spit dirt up. i throw dirt at the glass boy spinal cord and the glass boy spinal cord twitches with happiness. it pulls away from my neck and digs its tip into the dirt. it throws dirt in the air. [i am a father, the glass boy spinal cord says. after all those years stuck in a tiled floor, i am finally a father.] the glass boy spinal cord twitches again. it opens its bones and ingests the dirt clots. i flick the bones several times until the calcium comes apart and dirt flows out of the opening. [no dirt for you, i say] and the glass boy spinal cord pouts. it scoops the dirt up and holds it against its bony belly until the dirt stains the white parts dark brown. [the dirt is my child and i deserve to love it for as long as i want to, the glass boy spinal cord says.] it knocks its cord against the ground and the dirt jumps around. several pieces cling to the spinal cord. [are you hungry, the glass boy spinal cord asks.] [no, i am not, i say.] the glass boy spinal cord digs in the dirt. it throws the dirt over its head. it spears the dirt with an iron lung and the dirt settles into the ground. [you can't collect it, i shout. the dirt isn't yours. i birthed it. the dirt belongs to me.] red eyes push out of the hilltop walls. they linger over the dirt, prodding each particle out of the clot. individual dirt rocks roll beneath my back. the dirt lifts me up. the dirt hums and waves. it moves my back up and down. my bones click. my body aches. gray sores cover my arms and legs. [the birthing is done, the glass boy spinal cord says. you should feel proud. you have done your feminine duty.] i tear the glass boy spinal cord off my neck. i jam it into the dirt. [dig your way out, i say.] dirt collects on the spinal cord's top.

i, the BLOODLESS

GIRL, humming in a violent orange night: if you give me dirt again, i will eat each earthen cluster until you wish you had never had progeny. and i will bleach them until sugar white. GLASS BOY SPINAL CORD, afraid for its soul and the constant vinegar presence beneath its knees: you know better than to threaten me. i do not have the meat you require to survive. in fact, i have no meat at all. i am bone without any chance at restitution. and if we require our wrists to make a sacrifice, then yours are the first to go. BLOODLESS GIRL, digging her fingers in the dirt until mandrake roots bloom in her fists: i've known spineless skeletal pumpkins and cruel devil trees and worse BABA women and cannibal JERSEY DEVILS along with an assortment of angry pig faces and pink eye orbs and each was better than you would ever be, while combined they are the greatest mass i have ever known. GLASS BOY SPINAL CORD: your knees sicken me. BLOODLESS GIRL: i don't mean to be so dusty. but a dry thickness fills my throat and i cannot do a thing to rid myself of it. GLASS BOY SPINAL CORD: you have a deficit you need to come to terms with. BLOODLESS GIRL: i wasn't the one locked in a concrete floor for centuries. you should have freed yourself then. my greatest regret is ever agreeing to marry you. your flesh stinks of pickled rot and hard-boiled white shells push out of your eyes. i cannot stand the scent or look of you. you sit in the corner, spitting fur off your tongue and it makes my stomach sour. disgusting piece of flesh, monstrous little twerp. GLASS BOY SPINAL CORD: i gave you everything a wife could ever want. i gave you meat and red eyes. i gave you winged fiends and palatial towers reaching past the carnivorous stars. i gave you my skin to wear. and then you torture me? i don't understand what i gave you that was so wrong. BLOODLESS GIRL: you gave me pregnancy! GLASS BOY SPINAL CORD, moving his ribs like a snake: it was a gift. now we can remain connected for the rest of our lives. BLOODLESS GIRL: i can't get to the slaughter place if i have to worry about dirt. dirt can't follow me through the pine lands and the many drowning rivers. dirt can't help me through a glass maze with shards trying to cut my limbs off my body. and dirt cannot help me bathe in the blood-filled aluminum tub. dirt can absorb the blood though. dirt can take the blood away so that when i sink into the tub, it would be like sinking into quicksand. GLASS BOY SPINAL CORD: so sad. so very sad. all i wanted was to love you until you loved me back. but you hate me. you tore me out of my skin and wore me like a chain and you still can't love me. it isn't fair. none of it. it makes me sick, how you insist on pulling your affection away. just love me. or i will find the aluminum tub myself and steal the blood away. BLOODLESS GIRL: you wouldn't dare. i'll eat you if you try. i'll swallow each bone one at a time, then slurp the cord. GLASS BOY SPINAL CORD: exactly what i want! to be within you. i'll wind around your liver until rooted into place. try to pass me then. try. BLOODLESS GIRL: all i need is a scalpel and a pair of heavy tongs. GLASS BOY SPINAL CORD: i have several metal instruments growing in my tongue.

in the dusty

hilltop i play with my veins. they wriggle and wiggle around my flesh until i vomit. [is this morning sickness, i ask] and the dirt clumps settled in around me shake their particles. [no sickness for you, they chorus. good as new. you, you, you. that is why we loooooove you. will you give us a suckle of your breast?] the dirt leaps at my breasts. i throw a cup of liquor over their muddy surface. [no touching, i say. it's not allowed. i never said yes. and if you touch me again, i'll pave you over with molten concrete.] the dirt slumps down. the dirt stares at the floor-boards and whimpers loudly. [give us some mud, the dirt says.] [some mud, i ask. you're already mud. look at yourselves. dirty all around. my muscles aren't even that rancid.] the dirt sighs. the dirt grunts and heaves its body in my direction. i push the dirt away. i toss the dirt at a sour wall and break through. the wall groans. [how did you get inside, the dirt asks.] [inside what, i ask.] i push my fingers into the walls and hard enam-el flakes around my nails. the dust catches the sediment. my stomach aches. dirt pushes into my veins and travels through my muscle. [stop touching, i say.] i jab stainless steel needles into my wrists and catch the dirt particles on the ends. [come out, i whisper. come out. come out.] dirt clings to the metal and slides out of my skin. i twist my wrists in a backwards motion and my bones snap. dirt pours out. i would rather have dust than dirt. the glass boy spinal cord lengthens its body. it drapes off my shoulders. [we are hungry, hungry monsters, the glass boy spinal cord says.] [how many stomachs do you really have, i ask.] the spinal cord slumps. it thumps against my spine several times. my bones ache. red eyes blink above me. they burn through the hill ceiling and cluster together. [none, the spinal cord whispers. i cannot eat. i am a single organ mass incapable of ingestion.] i pat the spinal cord gently. the red eyes drift off to one side. they settle on the nearest wall and slump down to the floor. a red stain covers the wall behind them. the glass boy spinal cord leans away from me and swipes its tip through the red stain. [tomato juice, the glass boy spinal cord asks. pomegranate preserves? red grape marmalade? cherry jam? strawberry gelatin? bloody jelly? i do not know. but it tastes like scarlet sugar. i like the way it feels on the yellow marrow cord.] i dust the dirt away from me. [is there an afterbirth i should worry about, i ask.] the red eyes blink rapidly. [of course, the dirt clumps shout. there is always afterbirth! ours is sludge. beautiful, iron-filled sludge. open your mouth to receive it.] the dirt paws at my face. [afterbirth comes out not in, i say.] the dirt drops to the floor. pale gray sludge drains out of my knees. clumps drop onto the dirt and mix with the dry particles. [there, i say. all the children are born.] i lean to one side. i hold my hands over my mouth and breathe into my palms. the glass boy spinal cord strokes the sides of my neck gently, smoothing my skin. [you have never looked so beautiful, the spinal cord croons. we know you hate us because we are made of the glass boy but you are still beautiful with post-labor glow.] the glass boy spinal cord rests on my chest. i place my hands on the knotted tip. i sleep in the dirt.

i hold my

glass boy husband's spinal cord in my liver. the cord snakes around my innards, turning my wrists to meat and crying softly whenever it stands close to a marrow basin. [do you like yellow, the spinal cord asks.] but my husband is just being polite. he is not a good husband, but at night he feeds me forbidden fruits stolen out of a gutted factory's industrial abdomen. [you must eat something, my spinal cord husband says. or else you'll be weak.] my spinal cord husband worries about me. he lifts my hair and touches the back of my neck. the hilltop settles around me. dirt collects in my palms and kneecaps. [i can't stand the gristle, i whisper and the spinal cord husband sighs.] he slithers up my stomach and pulls my skin until it plucks like a string. i make music with my kidneys. i make the music loud and i make the music softly and when the music is done saturating my abdomen, then i eat the music up. it tastes like meat. many things taste like meat. even certain plants. then you don't have to deny your body the meat taste when opting for a wholly vegetarian diet. i am heavy with nonsense. the more i speak, the more swollen my arteries become until my circulatory system is drowned with dirt clots. the tubes do not asphyxiate. i do not allow it. but they can drown and so they do, taking in all the dirt they can then vomiting it back up. dry drowning. the same as a death by meat hook. but you cannot trust me when i say my bowels are irregular. i store the organs in a rusted pot and sprinkle dust over the top every morning. dust keeps meat from soiling. otherwise blue mold will coat the skin and every bite will have a sour fungal taste. i roll in the dust. i sweep the dust into my thighs and walk slowly. dust grains slide along my muscles, picking up spare bits of meat and taking them along, rolling each muscle in a thin coat of dust until i am a woman made of dust meat. i must not forget that i am blood-less. i am the most bloodless girl that has ever existed and if i had any blood at all, i would pour it into a golden chalice and drink. but there is no blood and there is no water and there is no bile. there are no fluids at all and i am tired of always being so dry. the dust grates against me. the dust bites my skin. the dust leaves holes in my muscles. i do not know where the dust starts and the meat ends just as i am confused as to when the meat starts and the dust ends. both seem to go on forever. both run up and down my bones while i force feed my liver pills of various oils taken out of a slaughterhouse floor. [you are the most beautiful bloodless girl in the world, the dirt says.] but i am not. i am the only bloodless girl. so when i give birth, it is to dust. and when i urinate, the waste is dust as well. and when i vomit, more dust. and when i ache from a kidney stone, that is also clotted dust. i push dust with dust. i make dust with dust. i eat dust with dust. my tongue swells with dust and that is how i digest. dust pushing dust down my esophagus until i choke. dust in my liver. my liver is open. my liver is open. my liver is open. my liver is open. my liver is open. my liver is open. my liver is open. my liver is open. my liver is open. my liver is open. my liver is open. my liver is open. my liver is open. my liver is open. and then it is not.

i and a

stomach removed from deep within the rotten dirt found
below the glass boy hang onto a door frame constructed of
porcupine splinters. [are you miserable, the stomach asks]
and tears ribs out of its narrow flesh throat. bones fall to the
floor. i touch the coiled husband spine around my neck and
the bones stir beneath my fingers. [do you love us, the bones
chorus. do you love us like a wife loves her husband? then we
will bite you until you turn colors. purple for you. purple!] i
push molten marrow into the bones. fatty resin solidifies in
the pores, clogging the bony voices. the stomach drags its bulk
across the floor. [i have too much meat within me, the stomach says.] [you are dust. just dust, i say.] the stomach sighs. it
spits fluid out of its tubes and wets the floor. [do you see any
meat within the bile, the stomach asks.] it flattens its bulk on
the ground and heaves back and forth several times. the stomach sighs and throws its tubes at the opposite walls. [you can
eat part of me if you'd like, the stomach says.] i step over the
stomach and the bones crush against my breast. [no, i say. i'm
not hungry. i think i need to follow the road outside. i need to
reach the blood-filled tub.] the stomach sits up. bile spurts out
of its bottom. [but that's the miserable road, the stomach says.
it is pockmarked with gray death. and it will tear your face off
if you turn the corner the wrong way.] i scratch the wall closest to me. bricks crumble in my hands. they fall to the ground.
mortar turns to powder. i put my eye to the thinning wall and
look through. white light shines back at me. [i need to get to
the slaughter place, i say. i keep forgetting that the aluminum
bin calls me. if i don't soak in the tub before the next harvest,
my limbs will stay dusty forever.] the stomach flops on the

floor and grunts. [we like you better dusty, the stomach says.] [that's what everyone tells me, i say.] i press my hands against the wall and climb up the brick. the wall falls beneath me. it follows. a small space opens. [there, i whisper. i can fit through.] the stomach sags. its tubes wrap around my ankles and yank me back. [don't go to the sad road, the stomach says. monsters beyond the bend will eat you. they'll skewer your stomach with onions and burned grass.] [i have enough stomachs to share with any cannibals, i say.] i push through the opening. the bricks gap and gape. they squeeze my sides. i fall out and the wall bricks up behind me. [please don't go, the stomach cries.] its longest tube pushes out of the bricks. the wall closes over it. the tube fidgets and falls limp with death. the road glimmers. i walk forward. all the roads look the same, like heavy mother worms made of stone and tar. they stretch and sometimes they resemble my head. but i do not know them. although i pity them. i've pitied them for the longest time. i crawl into the road. the asphalt cracks beneath my body. the glass boy spinal cord pulls out of my skin. [it will eat you, the bones scream. a terrible mouth of wretched teeth lives beneath the street.] the bones yank my neck. they pull me towards the curb. i flick the bones. [please, they cry, chipping at the enamel fragments stuck in their pores. the monster will devour us all.] i crack my fists. i crawl slowly and the road yanks at my shins. my legs dangle in the asphalt. but the road has a gray glow and my eyes tear joyously.

long before i

knew salt and sinew, my mother worm threw me in an aluminum tub filled to the top edge with boiling blood. [what if
i drown, i asked.] mother worm rubbed the top of my head
gently, pouring the blood over my forehead. blood ran down
my face and puddled up on my lap while the mother worm
flicked her segmentation around, sighing through her wide
circle mouth. [you cannot drown in anything pulled out of the
anatomy, the walls whispered.] mother worm peeled her rough
skin and threw meat onto the floor. she shook the last of the
dry flesh into a pile on the dirty tiled ground. i watched meat
slide and fall with a rustling sound. [are you going to eat me,
i asked.] mother worm shook her tail wildly. walls leaned over
the tub. they plucked salt grains out of the aluminum bottom
and held crystals over my head. [she would never eat you, the
walls said. that would be filicide. and why would your mother
commit such a taboo crime?] walls ingested the salt grains until
my mouth tensed with saline. i spit in the blood. the tub over-
turned, flooding everything with red fluid. the mother worm
floated to the top of the bath and wrung her pink flesh out
until the tips dried. [you have hurt the mother worm, the walls
said.] wet plaster patches dropped off their long sides. the plaster struck the floor and shattered into thousands of pieces. i
watched the patches grow and break apart. i twirled the wet
drywall around my fingertips in long sheets then pulled them
off with my front teeth. [there is another bath. it is in the basement, the walls said.] the mother worm sat up. blood drained
out of her skin. the mother worm clucked her wooden tongue
several times. she dug through the floors and slipped beneath
the boards. the walls shoved me. [you must follow, they said.

wherever the mother goes, so must you.] the walls went flat. i went under the floor and the mother worm forced her way from beam to beam, her stomach sagging and her spinal cord dragging behind. she paused in a small space and looked up. i sat beside her. rancid blood dripped onto my head. i wiped the blood away, but the blood fell faster. it dripped into my eyes. my vision turned red. the blood dropped onto my tongue and i tasted fresh copper notes. the blood hissed and squealed. the blood turned inside out and developed a sour milk texture. the blood was milk. it milked out of the walls. i closed my eyes. i pushed my fingernails into my tongue. but the blood flow kept coming. the blood came out of my hands. [but mother, i have enough fluids, i said] and the mother worm bled over me. her blood filled my lap. her blood sucked into my stomach. [i have enough fluids, mother, i screamed] and my mother worm paused with her mouth open, blood sagging near the back of her throat, blood waves sloshing from one side to the next. she coughed blood over me. i covered my face. blood stained my spine and my bones. it flowed until my muscle seized. mother worm turned. she pulled an aluminum vat out of the wall and yanked it towards me. she nodded her head and i pulled my dripping body over the edge. blood filled the tub quickly. it crusted along the sides. my bloody throat ached. i stayed in the aluminum vat. but i do not remember this until my dirt children remind me.

a woman stands

in the middle of the road. she pulls her grayish hair in front of her mouth, hiding her nose. the woman nods frantically. i stop near the road edge and stare at her. [do you need help, i ask] and the woman nods again. she turns slightly and points at the dead grass over the road edge. the grass waves back and forth, dead grains paddling in the earth. [i'm not a gardener, i say] and walk to the road's center. but the woman oinks. she oinks like a pig. she oinks so loudly my heart stops. i smack my fist into the meat and cough loudly. the woman drops her hair from her mouth. [but you're a pig, i whisper.] the woman nods. [how is that possible, i ask.] the pink eye orbs tucked into my stomach orbit around my kidney stones. [how is anything possible, they ask. you are bloodless. and a strange stone goat flies through the air. and she is a goat woman. you shouldn't judge. no, you should not. you are the strangest thing in these woods. who is bloodless anymore? bloody, yes. but not bloodless. it makes no sense. but you exist. and so should she.] the pink eye orbs settle their eyes in the kidney mass and silence their tongues. their eyelashes flutter. i pat my stomach and the pink eye orbs fall asleep. the pig woman stares at me. i look at her hands. they have fully formed fingers and long-boned wrists. her ankles are jointed. wooly socks cover her feet and it is better that i don't have to see her toes. she blinks so quickly her eyes grow sores across the retinas. [i'll help you, i say. i don't know where you want me to go. or what you expect me to do.] the pig lady points across the field. she heaves herself into the grain mass and runs on four legs, her swollen stomach pushing the grains down until they are flattened into rough cakes. i step into the grains and follow her slowly, tiptoeing around the wheat. [but you cannot trust her, the glass boy spinal cord hisses.] it dips past my shoulders and each bone snatches a piece of hay. the grain pushes through the calcium and hangs out of the pores. [do you like the way this flesh works, the glass boy spinal cord asks. of course not. you are listening to a porcine woman. she might as well be a cow. if only she had spots instead of so much pink flesh. we could eat her, just throw her onto a polished grill and let her roast until the bacon runs out of her fatty sides. she would crisp like a cracker. it must be the most delicious meat in the world.] the glass boy spinal cord sighs. it snaps like a whip. but i do not feel the bones cut me. i hear only the sound then a moment of coolness on my skin. nothing else. no welts. nothing. i look at my arms. there aren't any bruises. far away, nearly concealed by the moving grains, the pig woman raises her head and squeals. she gestures for me to follow. the glass boy spinal cord licks his bones. [so hungry. most delicious meat in the world, the glass boy spinal cord says.] i snatch a grain and shove it down the main cord line. the spinal cord goes quiet. i move the grains away from my waist. the pig lady hops up and down on her back ankles. she squeals and points past the grains. i step in front of her. i see gold. and grains. and dirt. and then, the sun flashes. silver flashes back. i narrow my eyes. i bite my tongue. tucked into the grass, concealed by dirt and mud, is a silver door. [the slaughter place, i ask.]

i think i

find the slaughter place. it has the same doors, a similar rusted exterior. but it is not the slaughter place because i have not given the proper sacrifice to touch its sides yet. the pig woman shakes. she bites the door handle with her tongue and wrenches it open. the pig woman nods her head, gesturing for me to step forward. [do not go, the glass boy spinal cord cries. do not walk first.] but i do. i walk first. i pause in the foyer and wait. the pig lady scrambles in after me. she closes the door. she snorts in my ear. her snout pushes against the back of my neck, shoving me forward. i walk slowly holding my hands out so my fingers drag across the walls. [are there bodies stuck in the walls, i ask.] but it is dark so i cannot tell if the pig lady shakes her head or nods. she oinks and shuffles down the hallway. the ceiling is lower than the slaughterhouse. there are too many rooms. the walls are made of brick. [this school is unsuitable for any of the children i have known, i say.] the glass boy spinal cord clings to my throat. [do not go, it whispers in my ear. do not go, do not go, do not go. what if she eats you? she looks hungry enough to bite her own stomach for the meat. do not go.] the spinal cord curves around my neck. i pull it back slightly. [you have to stop, i whisper. you aren't behaving.] [does misbehavior count as warning you not to get eaten, the spinal cord asks.] it slips down my collar bone and latches onto the slight hollow. damp mold drips off the ceiling and falls past my head. it strikes the floor and splatters. the spinal cord unwinds slightly and leans down, lapping moss up with the tip of its marrow points. the pig woman grunts again. she oinks and the sound carries down the hallway. it echoes around the corner and moves on. the pig lady runs. her feet smack against the stone floor and clomp down the walkway. the spinal cord pushes its marrow parts into my thighs and moans. [do not go, the glass boy spinal cord whispers. do not go. my beautiful wife, do not go. she will eat you up like a wolf eats a girl swathed in red hoods.] i press my fingers against the largest bone, hushing the spinal cord. the bone cord strains against my fingers for several minutes then relaxes, exhausted from straining. i breathe deeply and turn the next corner. i step into reddish light. the pig lady stands in front of me, her snout spread in a wide grin. her tiny black pig eyes glimmer with the faint red light. she twitches until her stomach falls apart. [it is time, she cries. it is better now. i can eat the raw flesh.] her molars crunch together. the spinal cord screams. [we told you, the bones shout.] they snake into my belly button and fill my spleen. a dull pain rises up my abdomen. i lean over and grunt softly. [it hurts, i whisper.] the pig lady smiles. [of course you hurt, she says. i have to cook you from the outside first. that leaves your meat with the slightest tinge of heat but not enough to ruin the muscle. now come here. i have a mouth waiting to chomp down on you.] the pig lady moves her jaws in a circle. her jaws rise and fall, rise and fall, rise and fall. they expand until they block off the reddish light. i back away. my arms brush over the nearest wall. green moss clings to me. i rub my hands over my arms quickly, knocking the wet fungus off. [don't touch me, i cry.] the moss strikes the floor and fills long spaces between the dirty bricks. the pig lady oinks again. [what if i eat you first, i shout.] i mash the flesh between my fingers and wait.

but i, trapped
in molten flesh, can only prod the walls with my tongue while
the pig woman bats the ground away. [you cannot harm me,
she screams and beats the brick.] it shatters into hundreds of
stone pieces while she watches with her beady eyes half-closed.
i loosen the spinal cord knot on my shoulder. the glass boy
spinal cord lifts up at the ends and glances in my direction.
[we must go back, it says.] [we must eat, i whisper] pointing
at the pig lady's stomach. the glass boy spinal cord shudders
slightly. [eat, he asks.] [eat, i say.] the spinal cord snakes off my
neck. he drops to the ground and slides along the floor, bones
tearing the rock into pieces. the pig lady looks down. [a snake,
she asks. how did you get down here?] she stoops over and
touches the spinal cord. the bones grab her fingers and shake.
her bones snap. fingers suck into the bone marrow. [you can't
stop the bones from eating, i say.] the pig lady drapes the spinal cord over an unused doorway and rattles the bones several
times. [i'll eat you first. maybe treat you like oyster shells with
some soy sauce splashed onto the pulp. do you taste like beef
or seafood, she asks.] the pig lady bites her knuckles. [the pig
has knuckles, the spinal cord whispers. pig knuckles!] the spinal
cord unwinds and bursts forward. he grabs the woman's stomach and tears the meat to pieces. bacon slabs strike the floor
and burst outward. i smell smoked meat. the pig lady digs her
fingers into her stomach and holds the falling bacon in place.
[don't go, she shouts] grabbing the meat. red meat clings to
her palms. the pig lady moves her hands back and forth, trying
to force the meat off. but her meat does not want to leave. it
holds tightly. the glass boy spinal cord stretches its cord. [time
for food, the spinal cord says.] he dives at the meat and tears

bacon out of the pig lady's hands. raw meat strikes the walls and drips to the floor. the spinal cord scoops and swallows. i edge around the massacre, my back flat against the wall, and when i reach the unused doorway, i pause near the frame and step through. the pig lady screams. [where does my meat go now, she asks. i was promised meat from a whole corpse. but the body lied. the meat escapes.] i pause. my feet scrape over the floor. i turn around. [what did you say, i ask.] the pig lady snaps her narrow jaws shut. she squeals deep in her throat. the spinal cord slashes her stomach apart and swallows the thick pork loins hanging onto her bowels. [you said you were promised meat, i say. who promised you meat?] the pig lady shakes her head. i point at the spinal cord. [eat her neck, i say.] the pig lady clicks her jaws together. the spinal cord pulls out of her stomach and snakes up the body, bones scabbing over and clacking. the pig woman rolls her eyes and whimpers. the spinal cord lingers near her jutting cheeks and rears back to take a bite. [the shadow, the pig lady whispers.] the spinal cord darts forward. i grab the spinal cord base and tug. the spinal cord strikes the floor and snatches at the passing stones. i wrap the cord around my neck. [what shadow, i ask.] the pig lady sighs. she moves her tongue up and down, testing the air with a reptilian manner. [what shadow, i ask again.] the pig lady pats her tongue gently. [the worm shadow ruining the slaughter place, the pig lady says] and swallows. i remember a shadow in the blood times.

maybe i touched
the slaughter place once before. or maybe the mother worm
dragged me into the dark bowels to live near the aluminum tub,
which was empty instead of filled with blood, and the more i
paddled my hands through the invisible water, the heavier my
fleshy pulp became. and i strained against the wrinkled flesh
but no amount of pushing would drain the water. the water
pained me. because the basement was so dark i could not tell
if i touched water or blood. there was no smell. there was no
color. there was only an invisible fluid that ran down my palms
and puddled up in the two-bone junction on my wrists. the
mother worm stayed near the stairs. she clung to the railing
and stared up the staircase. shadows passed over her body.
shadows moved back and forth, sliding instead of walking.
and once, the shadows paused near me but the mother worm
crunched her bowels together, forcing the shadows to leave.
so i slipped into the tub and watched the shadows sink into
the walls, floors, and a small rusted furnace at the center of
the room. [will the shadows haunt me forever, i asked] and the
mother worm nodded. she did not leave her wooden step and
the longer she stayed, the more her mucus-covered body fused
with the oak plank. [are you dying, i asked] and the mother
worm shook her head. i did not know salt then. i did not know
salt for many years. i did not know blood or slaughter places
or glass boy spinal cords or skeletal pumpkins or women with
pig features trying to tear raw meat from my stomach. i just
knew the basement and the mother worm. i slid in and out
of the aluminum tub, my hands numb from clinging to the
metal sides and the mother worm gazed up the stairs for hours,
her eyes rotten around the centers no matter how much white

vinegar she poured into the gelatin. [mother worm, are you decomposing from the inside out, i asked] and mother worm poured gallon-sized bottles of vinegar down her long throat. vinegar pickled her innards. she smelled like brine. when she squirmed, a sweet salt mixture flowed out of her skin and wet the floor. [can i have some mother, i asked] and the mother worm directed the stream at me. i cupped my hands together. i drank until my stomach ached with moisture. i grunted and mother worm squirmed over my back. she rubbed my spinal cord. i looked around the basement and a rotten stench came out of the walls. it bubbled and flowed down the radiators. i waved my hand in front of my face, trying to fan the scent away, but the smell came out of the walls and forced its way through my skin. rotten sinew dropped out of me. meat struck the floor and died, caustic bile running out of the strands until tiny holes formed in the concrete slabs. i watched and the mother worm covered my eyes with her body. she wound her anatomy around my head and held on tightly. i heard holes burning and the radiator humming until it burst. metal dripped off the walls and puddled up in the aluminum basin, overflowing the moisture already inside. [has the bath been ruined, i asked]. [you'll find another one, the mother worm said. and it will be a bath of blood made for you to bathe in. you must sink to the bottom. you must let the blood flow in.]

i leave the

pig lady alone. she salivates over her hoofs, crying until pink saliva runs down her face. [the shadow will eat me now that you know, the pig lady shouts and slams her hoofs against the walls.] the glass boy spinal cord tightens around my neck. [do not listen, the spinal cord says. move forward. move forward.] the spinal cord pushes my spine, urging me forward. we leave red light. we leave the pig lady behind and she falls to the floor. the spinal cord closes the metal door. [i don't know where to go now, i say.] i close my eyes and try to see the aluminum tub with its metal smell, but all i see is the worm shadow. the spinal cord snakes off my shoulders until he dangles from my lower arms. [you'll find the way, the spinal cord says. just sniff it out. you should be able to do that. just sniff your way from this hovel to the place above. you'll smell the red scent soon. then you can locate the slaughter place.] i walk slowly. my feet sink into dark mud. hard objects rise to the surface and knock against my ankles. [do not go any farther, the objects whisper.] they have wispy voices that vibrate in my lungs. i close my eyes and step forward. i crush an object into the ground. [what are they, i ask.] the spinal cord shivers. [roast loins, he says. but not the good meat kind. one that craves meat of its own.] the spinal cord twitches and i yank the tail slightly. an object resembling a femur lifts out of the mud and bites my foot. it draws dust. my meat hangs off my bones. splitting pain travels up my leg and it is like a seared burn without the charcoal center. i fall into the mud. the spinal cord drops off my neck and clatters away. he strikes the opposite wall and slides away. my hips sink into the mud. i squint and bones rise out of the muck. they grapple with my knees, yanking the skin down. i slide my hands through the mud, pushing them away. [don't bite, i whisper. don't bite.] i claw the mud and the bones bite my palms. meat hangs off my wrists. meat falls apart beneath my fingernails. the spinal cord twitches. the glass boy spinal cord crawls up the wall to the ceiling and hangs over my head suspended by its sticky bone fragments. [we'll save you, the spinal cord bones shout.] they dip down and swat the top of my head. the bones strike the side of my face. [that hurts, i shout.] the mud bones slither around me. they chop at my thighs. [let me go, i cry. i'm not meat.] the mud bones giggle. they open their outsides to expose the marrow middle. [meat meat meat, they sing and cluck their marrow against the calcium.] i push myself to my knees and force myself down the hallway. the bones pull at my back. they yank my legs out from under me. i fall repeatedly. my body sags. i groan and keep my head low. [you won't bite me again, i say.] but the bones bite me again. then again. and again until i am covered in dust and the mud is not as fluid. [get away, i whisper. get away.] my tongue catches behind my teeth and i reach the end of the hallway. the bones crack. they leap out of the mud and drop down heavily, landing flat on the hard surface. fractures run over the calcium. i swallow and my eyes ache. [do not be so scared of the shadows, the ceiling says. they only bite once. that is enough.] the glass boy spinal cord lets go of the ceiling. he lands on my head and curls up beneath my hair. i look back. the mud bubbles around its edges then crusts open. a staircase snarls.

slowly slowly the

glass boy spinal cord and i slide up a rancid staircase pock-marked with burned bits and smoldered edges. the metallic leviathan heaves beneath my feet and i cling to the railings. but the bars do not hold. they sway back and forth. one by one the bars snap off the rails and clatter to the hard mud below. i back away from the edge and touch the opposite wall. stable plaster presses against my back. the staircase shakes harder. [we'll fall over, the glass boy spinal cord cries. we'll die in the acid bath tucked beneath.] the spinal cord pierces my neck and jabs into the bone column. [there's no acid bath down there, i say. we were just there. it was mud. where did you think the acid would come from?] the spinal column looks at the ground. [maybe it was vomited, the glass boy spinal cord says.] it plays with its bones and i touch my fingers to my neck wound. [you shouldn't bite, i say. that isn't polite.] i release the bars and take the steps two at a time. we are only thirteen steps from the top. the glass boy spinal cord hangs down my neck. it grabs at the falling railings. [we will die if we keep going, the spinal cord cries. we will pitch off a step and fall. do you know what happens when meat smacks against concrete?] the spinal cord tightens its grip on me and i rub my stomach gently, flattening the meat into a lightly packed steak. [stop complaining, i whisper. the meat will be fine. the meat will be the greatest thing you have ever tasted. we have to reach the top.] the spinal cord twitches. he wraps around my shoulder blades and i run faster. i throw myself over the top landing and roll on the uneven floor. broken plaster flies at my face. i sit up and the stone shards land on the ground. the spinal cord gasps. [where are we now, the spinal cord asks.] i raise my head. a long hallway expands from the landing and twists from side to side, the walls overgrown with weeds and trees. plaster lies on the floor and several holes stare directly into the muddy basement below. i stand up and the spinal cord grinds against my vertebrae. [should we keep going, the glass boy spinal cord asks. we shouldn't. we should stay here in one place and resist the temptation to go any further. or else we will die. do you understand? we are close to death even standing in this hallway.] i squeeze the small nerves jutting out of the thick bone chunks. [be quiet, i whisper.] i step into the hallway. glass and concrete stones crunch under my feet. i pause in the first doorway on my left. rows of desks fill the room, facing a blackboard marked with white lines reading STAY OUT OF THE MUD. the spinal cord rubs its tip against the board and smears each T shape until it resembles a P. [they should have put the warning on the steel door. what good is it to be warned when we have already stumbled through the mud, the spinal cord asks.] the spine hangs down my shoulder and slumps onto the nearest desk. he thuds on the wood. i look past the desks. broken windows line the walls, the sills covered with greenery. i walk past the desks. [i don't like this room, the spinal cord says.] walls crumble around me. paint shreds roll to the ground. dust crunches. my fingers dance over the window frames. they swipe over the dust. the room rolls. [we should leave, the spinal cord says.] dust figures sit at the desks. and i am beginning to see.

mother worm was

not the only worm or the only mother or the only piece of skin embedded beneath my nails for the entirety of my life. [it is not normal to cry, mother worm said] with a nod of her segmented head and so i wiped my tears away. i cried at least twenty-five times a day and each cry was a terrible sob that forced my lungs to stop working. so my innards ached and the pain was so much that i tore my legs off and tossed them into the air. but mother worm stitched the legs back on. [no child of mine will go without legs, she said in my head] then cradled me to sleep. but mother worm was a liar. mother worm bled me dry because i kept a salt crystal tucked into the space between my breasts and i did not want mother worm to ply me with so many salty granules but she did. then mother worm nearly died and i was so frightened i let her ingest me. i lived in her stomach for one thousand days and each one was just as long as the last ones and every one after that stunk of sour things and i could not think of meat even though i wanted to desperately. later mother worm rested on the ground and wooden things tried to squish her. they drummed their wooden frames against her back until bile squirted out of her mouth. the death strokes. but she stayed alive for another thirteen years while i cleaned brown water off the tiles and gave the mother worm rancid food to eat. [mother worm, i whispered. will you kill me when i sleep?] mother worm did not answer. after that, whenever i touched a radiator it died a loud hissing death i could not stop. i placed pressure on the pipe joints but that did nothing. the steam hissed into my palms, burning my skin. boiled muscle slid up and down my bones. i could not stop the shuddering meat. i licked the cooked parts and spread them around the floor for the radiator to eat. [if you chew something, you might forget that you're dying, i said] and the radiator fell onto its side, spewing dirty water across the floor. mother worm picked me up by my hair. she swung me around and her small eyes went glassy and wild. she threw me into an aluminum bath and poured bleach over my stomach. mother worm scrubbed. mother worm rubbed broken skin off my muscle and tossed the useless pieces to the side. mother worm cried loudly while she worked. she pressed glass vials against my skin and collected all the moisture running out. [so you never go dry again, mother worm whispered into the glass] but mother worm could not speak out loud even though she moved her mouth up and down. mother worm hummed and mother worm reached around her back, grabbing for a spine that had never been there. mother worm wrapped her tail around my head and yanked me. she bled me into a cup then into a tub. the blood filled the tub to its very top metal and stayed beyond the boundaries. it rippled and threatened to spill over but never did. it was beautiful. i reached to touch the blood and mother worm smacked my hands away. [you cannot touch, the mother worm whispered in my throat. you still have fluid in you. you have to wait until you've gone dry. when will that be, my wet girl? when will that be?] she bit my throat and the blood flowed faster. it splashed the floor and wet everything. and i could not touch the aluminum tub.

my hair grows.

i, in a tower high above a school filled with vines and loose tree roots, watch the woods. the JERSEY DEVIL flies past me, its concrete tail whipping the topmost branches. leaves drift to the floor. branches crash to the ground. a headless torso pushes its way through the undergrowth and hums with its many stacked ribs. the sound pulses through the tree trunks and knocks several roots to the ground. [how hungry are you today, the spinal cord asks] and rises off the floor to snake around my ankle. i turn away from the broken windows. the headless torso dives through a basement window and clatters around in the hardened mud. [it will suffocate, the spinal cord whispers. a slow death but a necessary one.] the JERSEY DEVIL rests on the school ceiling and flaps its wings several times before lifting into the air. i sit on the floor. dust collects in my lap. powder forms the shape of my lap. the spinal cord drops into the dust center and throws the powder into the air. [it is better, the spinal cord screams. the mud lives.] i twirl my long hair around my wrists. i cover my arms with thick strands. the hair cuts into my skin and leaves burned marks on the flesh. i fall onto my side and breathe the dirt slowly. dust fills my lungs. a sharp aching feeling pulses in my stomach and i push my hands against my abdomen. an old woman with a hood over her face walks up the hallway, her feet dragging in the dust. she kicks powder up and into my face. i bat the powder away. [who are you, i ask] and the old woman pushes her hood down. a wide smile separates her face into two parts. [dear girl, these are my hallways, the woman whispers] and reaches out. her fingernails end in long claws that scrape my shoulders and upper arms, leaving deep red marks in my skin. [are you hungry, the woman asks.

i have meat to share, fine wines tapped directly from a grape skin. but it is not really a grape skin. it is something else, a monster with a wrinkled face and red flesh. but it is delicious. and intoxicating. you will like it, my darling child.] the spinal cord shrinks back. [do not eat her food, the spinal cord whispers.] the old woman pushes her tongue between her front teeth and hisses. [how dare you, she hisses. how dare you judge me? i am trying to feed this poor princess, alone in the dark with only a column of vertebrae for friends.] the spinal cord clenches my shoulders. it spits on the floor. i swallow dust. powder scrapes my throat dry. [would you like meat, the old woman asks.] her eyes bulge around the corners and yellow pupils push out of her eyes. [it is wet and raw. dripping with blood. you will like it. it tastes like good flesh, she whispers.] she lifts her hands to touch my wrists and i pull back. the JERSEY DEVIL roars. it beats its wings against the windows, shattering the last of the glass. [what is that beast, the old woman screams. what is that monster on my roof?] the old woman sprints to the hallway. her hood drops down to the center of her spine. golden braids sprout from her skin. [a monster, she screams. a monster in my tower. you cannot go until the monster is slain. kill it. i want to wear its skin.] the old woman pulls the plaster down. it falls on my back, pushing me to the floor. [you will stay. and we will feast on that monster for years, she says] and leaves me.

i am an

old woman's prisoner in the pastoral school. she limps around
a dusty room, throwing wooden chairs into the air and knocking them down with her feet. [i am hungry, she screams. where
is the meat?] attached to my neck, the glass boy spinal cord
sleeps soundly. the vertebrae tucked into a thick marrow bed
that ripples across its surface but does not drip. the old woman
hammers a mirror down its center. [is there meat in here, she
asks] and presses her face against the jagged glass shards. i get
onto my knees. i crawl across the floor slowly, dragging my
hands through the dust. powder hangs on my flesh. i creep
towards the walls and the old woman turns around. [where are
you going, she asks. we need to eat. we need meat. where is the
meat? where do we find the meat?] she smacks her fists against
the walls and knocks plaster to the floor. [do you know where
the meat is, the old woman asks.] she digs her fingers into my
back and drags my skin towards her palms. [i don't know where
the meat is, i whisper. let me go.] the old woman cracks her
jaws. [of course you do. you've been here forever. meat is in
the walls and you know where the best slabs are located. are
they tucked into the stairs? pushed into the floorboards? hidden in the basement? where can i find the meat, the old woman
asks. i am so hungry.] she nods her head frantically and her
lower jaws strike the ground. wood splinters fly into the air and
skewer the plaster near her face. i turn onto my side and kick
the old woman's stomach. my foot hits her fat and bounces
back. [i am a lard woman, she whispers.] she lifts the fabric on
her stomach and white lard drips out. it splatters the floor. a
rancid fat smell fills the air. i gag. [walking lard, i ask.] the old
woman smiles. butter sticks slide out her mouth and collect on

the floor between her feet. i watch the yellow mound grow. the old woman giggles into her knuckles. [i think you are just as hungry as i am, the old woman says. i know you have to be. i hear it in your stomach. because you are a ghost. as am i. hungry ghosts living in the bowels of this terrible pastoral school in constant search for steak. do you want steak, little girl? do you want a nice piece of meat in your stomach? will that make you happy?] the old woman tears her hands apart and tosses the meat onto the floor. [that's meat, i say.] i point at the red flesh sinking into the floorboards. juice drips between the slabs and strikes the basement floor. [foreign meat, the old woman screams. strange protein. i do not want steak pulled from my bones. i do not like it. i already know that taste.] fat puddles up on the old woman's open hands. she puts her palms to her lips and sucks the juice up. fat clings to her lips. her skin glimmers with fatty moisture. [it is so delicious, the old woman croons. would you like a bite?] the old woman scratches the sides of her face and fat comes out of the wounds. i look up at the dusty ceiling. i stare down at the dusty floor. [i think i know where the meat is, i whisper.] the old woman's lips open. she grabs her stomach and clenches the meat tightly. [i knew it, she cries. give me the meat then.] i point at a crack in the wall. [in there, i say] and kick coals away. the old woman throws herself at the crack. her head slips in, then her shoulders. i touch the wall. the hidden oven turns on. i watch ashes.

i eat dust.
i shove it down my throat and my neck strains against the powder. [you have to stop, the spinal cord cries] and pushes against my mouth. but i am hungry and desperate. i throw the glass boy spinal cord to the side. tilting my head back, i swallow the dust hanging off the ceiling. my stomach distends. my skin pulls free of my bones and lies against the floor, a meaty sack against the concrete. [you'll die, the glass boy spinal cord screams. stop eating the dust. you have enough shoved inside your muscles.] the spinal cord snakes towards me. i smack the bones hard. i shatter the lumbar region. the spinal cord limps. [but i am your husband, the spinal cord whispers. why would you injure me like this?] he breathes laboriously, bones wide with flesh and sinew. i pat the spinal cord gently. [i hate you, i whisper] and strip a bone off the nervous system. the spinal cord flops in the dust. i lift the removed bone to my mouth and lick thick dust off the edges. [but you married me, the spinal cord sighs.] i throw the bone to the floor and take another bone from the spinal cord. i place it on my tongue and chew slowly. acidic dust drains out of the bone marrow and settles inside my cheeks. it burns through my flesh. i spit meat chunks out. the spinal cord writhes. the end digs into the floor and roots between three metal rods. [you married me, the spinal cord screams] rising up. bones smack against my wrists, fracturing the thin bones. i stand up. dust pours out of my mouth and runs down the spinal cord. [i want a divorce, i say.] i spit dirt onto my feet and kick into the air. dust showers my face. it clings to the walls and veils the doorways with particles. [a divorce, the glass boy spinal cord asks. a divorce? you would ask me for a divorce? i love you.] i lift the spinal cord by his

marrow tip and whirl him around in the air. [you were beautiful when you were a glass boy and i released you from the floor. but i didn't love you. i loved the glass. and i do not love you. spinal cord monster. evil bone growth. marrow snake. jointed cannibal column. nervous system constrictor. you could never help me find the mother worm or the blood-filled tub. i will never love you. not after you cling to my throat and prevent me from breathing, i hiss.] i tear the spinal cord in two. the two ends twitch in my hands. they collapse on the ground in a fit of dust and dried protein. [you were the only wife i ever knew, the spinal cords whisper.] they touch marrow and sink into the concrete. a yellow stain forms over their bodies. i stand near the pigmentation and scratch my palms until my skin flakes off. whitish powder drifts onto the spinal stains and settles between the last bone fragments. i lean down and pick the stains apart. the color slips between my fingers and coats my skin. [i can't even say you were a good companion, i say. not when your every word made me sick with anger.] i kick the stains away. around me, the walls creak loudly. plaster falls down. in the hallway, chairs rattle. their legs snap in half and metal rolls up and down the floor, collecting dust along the tubes. i step into the hallway. pale yellow dust fills the room behind me. powder presses against my palms, shoving me into the hallway. i walk past the broken chairs and desks. wood collapses near my sides. [i think i am hungry, i say] and the walls open up into a gaping doorway.

i leave ovens,
lard women, and meat byproducts behind. i leave the spinal
cord husbands, glass shards, and mud basements. i leave the
bones, staircases, and ivy windows. i leave the skeletal pumpkin,
devil tree, and BABA woman. i leave the forest, concrete, and
paint. i leave everything but the dust. i return to the only road
i know and i walk slowly with my eyes aching and my hands
moving around in front of my eyes until i am so sickened by
the motion that i pause to stare at the moon, which looks like
the mother worm, only fatter. [how hungry are you now, i ask.]
the moon vomits blood red fluid onto the path in front of me.
[i am a dust girl. i can't touch any of your moisture, i say.] the
moon glares. the moon touches the dirt and the fluid hardens into solid red stone. [move on, the moon says] and i walk
slowly, edging around the fresh stone to reach the ground on
the other side. there are roads made of glass and roads constructed through hollow trees and roads picked together with
lunar stones. there are roads that resemble old bones and roads
that stink of rotten meat. there are roads that curve so dras-
tically that they resemble the glass boy's face. [did you know
him, i ask.] the moon smiles. [i put him in the ground, the
moon says. i placed the stones over his face one by one until
his smile sunk into his bones. and then i forced the rest down,
chiseling around the stones to make a hollow large enough to
accommodate many rusted nails. i did all of that because that
glass boy was too fragile and it sickened me. just as it sickened
you. don't you hate the way he looks watching you with all
his bones, telling you to go back, to stay away from the meat
source? all because he is afraid. he is a very scared little boy.
and you are a bloodless woman who shouldn't be chained to

a spinal cord.] the moon hisses between three front teeth and unravels a long red tongue that stretches across thirteen mountains and an ocean. [you can eat from the meat if you choose, the moon says] and picks at the tongue muscle. fibers snap. i watch the meat swell with internal bleeding. [i can't touch it, i say. there's too much fluid. and i have to stay away.] the moon leans down. the moon brushes against my skin. the moon is cold and a chill covers my arms. i pull away. the moon forces a smile across her solid stone and the rocks break between her teeth. [i knew your worm mother, the moon says. she was the greatest cannibal in all the land. but she never spoke. she opened her mouth and chewed but there were no sounds. there were no squeals, no yelps. barely any breathing. she lived to chew. and then she was salted. do you know who salted her?] the moon knocks against my shoulders and i lose my balance. [no, i say.] but i do know who salted my worm mother. i salted her and i would salt her again if i could because she bled me dry in the slaughter place and used the aluminum tins to collect my blood as a souvenir. [i miss my worm mother, i say] and the moon spreads her stomach wide, curling black flesh edges around the stomach hole. the moon gestures at the center pit. [climb in, she says. your mother worm is inside. she misses you. she thinks you have forgotten what she looks like. did you forget what she looks like?] i touch the stomach flesh. i lift up. the moon bowels swallow me. i crawl and everything inside looks like a worm.

i sort worms.

i sort them by length and color and girth. i stack worms until they reach the top of a cavernous moon mouth. then i knock the worms down and fill the moon's stomach with wormy flesh. [that is nice, the moon whispers. that is very nice. my bowels feel full. you are good for my body.] the moon reaches down her throat and pats the top of my head. i gag slightly. my eyes water. worms cling to the back of her tongue and she pushes them down with a fingernail. [i never used to eat worm meat, the moon says. it was always raw beef and maybe some steaks pulled out of a full-grown man. but not worms. they didn't seem meaty enough. but now i know. pure protein. they make my stomach sing. listen.] the moon presses a finger to my ear and points to her esophagus. gas wheezes over her tongue. digestive sounds echo and fluctuate. it sounds like music, terrible gaseous music that causes my stomach to ache. [heeeeeveee haaaaa hooooo eeeeeehhhhh haaaaaaa, the music whispers.] the moon kisses her fists. she strokes her tongue. i lift the worms up and toss them at her lips. the moon gags. [they cannot come out, she screams. leave them inside. they must go the opposite way past my teeth.] the moon licks her lips and the worms come apart on her tongue. the flesh slides down her throat and collects in her stomach pool. i shovel the rest of the worms, long blue fibers that resemble old veins and thicker red ones that should be entire steaks but are not because they are too tube-like. [do you know the slaughter place, i ask] and the moon rolls her eyes. i look at the top of her mouth and watch the backs of her eyes rock back and forth. they swivel and roll before dropping onto her tongue. the moon swallows her eyes. gelatinous orbs push past my legs and drop into her stomach.

they land on top of the worms and sink to the bottom of the squirming meat. [the slaughter place, the moon whispers. no one knows about the slaughter place.] the moon wipes her face with her hands and red marks cover her cheeks. [but i knew a staircase that knew the slaughter place, i say. but it died before it could give directions.] the moon sighs. sour breath moves up her throat and knocks against me. i fall onto her tongue and cling to the thick taste buds. saliva foams over me. [i think the slaughter place is far away, the moon says. so far away that you need to cut your fingers off to get there. because it is in a glass palace protected by cannibal birds swathed in ruby red feathers. and there are other bodies hanging from the sky, ready to tear your throat out if you get too close. you might be dust-filled but you still have meat.] the moon sniffs and her tongue strikes the top of her mouth, pushing me into the roof. i strike a small crevice and dig my nails into her rocky meat. i yank myself into the crevice and squirm across her meat. [that sounds like another story, i say. one about a little girl who accidentally cursed her brothers until they were black birds. and because she was so guilty, she went to an emerald palace to unlock their hearts.] the moon slaps her tongue again. wet flesh slides over my back. i crawl faster, my hands and knees sinking into her palate. i pull free of the moist flesh and bump my head against the back of her teeth. [what happened to my worms, the moon asks] tasting. i slip out. she ignores me.

i twine red

string around the moon's underside, latching the thread around
pustules growing out of her rocky flesh. the moon grunts and
pulls against me but the thread is heavy and strong. it pulls her
down. [is this a gravitational pull, the moon shouts. i do not
like this. i want to go back into the sky. where did the worms
go? i am so hungry.] the moon hangs low. her crescent slashes
through several dead trees. ash gray trunks crash to the forest floor. splinters spray against the moon's sides. she screams.
[there are nails inside of me, she cries. i have been stabbed,
slaughtered, raped. help me.] the moon fumbles with the splinters. she crushes them between her hands. [please, the moon
cries. please help me. i cannot get them out. they break in my
fingers. and they hurt so terribly.] the moon moans softly. she
pulls at her body and sighs as the splinters snap. i tug the red
thread and the moon drifts behind me. she smacks into tree
branches and wooden limbs crack in half. [i want to go back
into the sky, the moon says.] [no, i say.] [but i cannot stand the
way this ground smells, she says.] [i don't care, i say. i'm keeping you and you're going to help me get to the mother worm.]
[but if i am down here, i cannot light anything, she says.] [it
is nighttime. there doesn't need to be light, i say.] [but there is
light, she cries. there is too much light. it is everywhere. it looks
like daylight because i am so close to the dirt. what if the dead
rise because they think it is morning? what if they claw out of
the dirt and bite?] the moon strains against the string. i wind
the loose end around my wrist and knot it behind my thumb.
[you're my celestial pet now, i say.] the moon moans. she sticks
her tongue out and the meat drags across the dirt, collecting
earth on the tip and scooping it back towards her throat. [you

have to let me go, the moon says. i do not belong down here.] i whip the thread and a strong vibration travels from the string to the moon. the moon trembles. [this is not right, the moon says. this is not right at all. why would you hurt me? what did i do to you? i carried you in my jaws lovingly. i did not eat you.] i whip the thread again and the moon bobs up and down. her body strikes the ground and rises up. [please stop, she begs.] i snap the thread one last time and adjust the knot again. [you swallowed my mother worm, i say. i know you did. i found her bones.] the moon opens her jaws and snaps them shut. [you found her, the moon asks. how did you find her? i kept the bones tucked into my stomach so deeply, they could never be uprooted without my feeling it. the bones are part of me. how did you get them out without forcing my red fluids to the surface?] the moon lifts her tongue and holds it in front of her face. [i knew you ate my worm mother, i say.] [you found her bones. of course you know, the moon moans.] [i never found her bones. i lied, i say.] the moon tucks her tongue back into her stomach and breathes quietly. her eyes illuminate with a pale green. she plays with her fingers and the tips break off. [what will you do with me, the moon asks.] her cheeks break as she speaks. i stare at her overhanging stomach and press my finger into her flesh. i feel the cratered meat for my mother worm's bones. [you'll bring me to the slaughter place, i say. i have to find the blood-filled tub.] the moon bleeds. [then i'll take my mother worm back, i say.]

i and the

moon, hand in hand, through a landscape of bone and archi-
tecture. the moon hits her stone against heavy towers rising
through a smoggy atmosphere to reach dark stars hanging
above. [i should be up there, the moon sobs into the string]
soaking the line with her saliva. i flick the thread up and down
several times until the fluid dries. [are you trying to hurt me, i
say. you know i can't touch moisture. you must be moistening
me intentionally. do you think i'll drown?] the moon trembles.
i feel her shuddering through the lines. [how far away is the
slaughter place, i ask.] the moon sighs. [it is through the trees
and up a large hill, she says.] [is it a hollow hill or a filled one, i
ask.] the moon cringes. she grabs a tree branch in her jaws and
it snaps in half. [i am tired of talking, the moon screams] and
curls her lips away from her teeth. i throw a stone at the center of her front teeth and break two fangs. [too many people
keep me away from the slaughter place, i say. i am so tired of
dreaming about it at night. i know i was there once before. my
mother worm brought me. did she tell you that before you
chewed her? she brought me to bleed me dry. my blood is in
those aluminum vats. and i need to bathe to be whole again.]
the moon spits on the ground. she burns a hole through the
dirt. i turn my head to one side and the brown earth fizzles.
[how sad, i whisper. i have bones stored down there i might
have fed you if you hadn't been so spiteful.] the moon shows
her tongue. [put that meat away. you might attract lard women,
i say.] i yank the string towards me and the moon drops out of
the sky. she strikes a tree and falls to the ground. dirt clings to
her bony body. the moon smacks her tongue against her sides
and scrapes gravel away. [i do not like this, the moon moans.

i do not like this at all. there shouldn't be any sinew outside my body. there shouldn't be dirt at all. make the dirt go away. why can't i go back into the sky? i lied. i never ate your mother worm. i swear i never ate her. she chased me across a desert and tried to skin me alive.] the moon flings herself at a puddle and douses her face with dirty pond water. [all that algae is worse than any dirt you've touched, i say. i don't believe you. my mother worm is a terrible worm but she is not a cannibal.] the moon slurps the water up and vomits several tons of orange digestive bile. [she is a cannibal, the moon sobs. she is a cannibal. she ate me in pieces. then she threw me up.] the moon rolls onto her back. i pull the string and the moon drifts across the water to me. [i want to return to the sky, the moon sobs. there are phases i haven't entered yet. i want to be a new moon.] the moon turns and grabs my hands. she clings to me and i push her back. the string frays. i tear my hair from my scalp and wind it around the thinning string. [if you bring me to the slaughter place, i might let you return to the sky, i say. but i need to bathe in my blood first.] the moon blinks rapidly. her stones change color from a slate gray to a pale periwinkle blue. [do you promise, the moon asks.] she tugs on the string gently, testing its strength. [it depends if i gain my moisture back, i say.] the moon releases the string. she floats upward. the string rises with her and goes taut. i check the knot around my wrist. i walk on. the moon drifts behind.

factories sprout behind
the moon. they grapple with metal towers and gnash their teeth
together until glassy concrete falls to the earth. windows reflect
the moon's face and she turns from side to side, trying to avoid
the doppelgangers. [i cannot stand the sight of that flesh, the
moon moans] and slashes her face with her tongue. i yank the
moon away from the buildings. [that isn't flesh. those are buildings, i say. stone. rock. glass. steel. but not flesh.] the moon rises
and falls. [make them go away, she whispers. i hate all those
hungry things. they look at me as if i am steak.] the buildings
tumble to the ground. steel cables snap and dig into the dirt
like roots. dust smears over the glass. slowly metal melts and
mixes with bole. [do we wait for the burial to complete, the
moon asks] and i tug the string again, yanking her past the
architectural burial ground. the moon winces. the thread cuts
through her stone and leaves deep red marks across her center.
[it is not right, the moon whispers. i did not mean to know
your mother worm. but she came to me.] [i don't care whose
fault it is. you're helping me get to the slaughter place and you'll
stop complaining about it, i say.] towers tumble and glass splinters pierce the moon's sides. [please let me go, the moon says.]
she sticks her tongue out and trips over the elongated muscle.
muscle, muscle everywhere and not a bite to eat. i sing nursery
rhymes in my head. [[[moonlight had a naughty skin, naughty
skin, naughty skin. moonlight had a naughty skin, it tied men
into bows. and everywhere that moonlight went, moonlight
went, moonlight went, everywhere that moonlight went, the
men were sure to go. they followed her to a slaughter place,
slaughter place, slaughter place. they followed her to a slaughter place and found a large red thing. all the hooked things bled

and sang, bled and sang, bled and sang, all the hooked things bled and sang to see the lack of skin. a bladed monster hanging down, hanging down, hanging down, a bladed monster hanging down, grabbed them by their meat. the hooked things shouted we must eat, we must eat, we must eat. the hooked things shouted we must eat but there was never food. why does moonlight love the men, love the men, love the men, why does moonlight love the men and bend their spines in half? the vertebrae snap apart, snap apart, snap apart, the vertebrae snap apart with a cracking sound.]]] the moon rises over a skyscraper. long vines twine around my string and i pull myself up the cord slowly, moving hand over hand until i reach the bottom of the moon. [i will shake you to the dirt, the moon shouts.] i reach around the navel bulge to snag the vines with my fingertips. they tug and catch between my fingers. i pull back. i force the vines down my wrist and into the small loop beneath my thumb. [i will toss you to the ground, the moon shouts.] the vines fray. i bite the loose ends and wood shatters between my teeth. [no you won't, i yell. you can't because if you let me go, i'll be holding onto the rope and you'll never get free. i sewed the rope into my skin. it's part of me.] i snap the vines and drop the string to the floor. it winds around its body, landing in a perfect mound. i slide down the rope. my feet touch the ground. the moon sighs. it smacks against a building and knocks the walls down.

with the moon

dragging behind me, i cross the stony road made of slate and mica sheets. the road curves to the right and i watch the corners closely. a figure swathed in gray gossamer stands just beyond the first curve, a light bulb pressed into a palm's center. [who are you, i ask] and stand in front of the figure. [someone you once knew, the figure says] and stoops over to touch the dirt floor. i step off the road and stand in the grass beside the figure. we watch the road for several minutes and the rocks settle into the molten innards before drifting back towards the sides. [were you family or friend, i ask.] the figure shrugs. [neither, the figure says.] [enemy, i ask.] the figure touches its filmy hood and tucks loose fabric folds beneath its chin. [no, the figure says. not an enemy. i might have been a blood connection.] the figure crosses its legs and sits on the ground. grass grows between its thighs and breaks its skin up with thick green patches. [i knew you a long time ago, the figure says. you were young. i knew the mother worm.] the figure sighs and the hood drops farther down its face until all i can see is a thin mouth moving up and down. the figure sticks a stick-like pink tongue out and bobs the tongue around in the air for several minutes, tasting water vapor and tiny protein particles glistening around its head. the moon stays just above the road, its bulbous form hovering just low enough to cast a long shadow across the next three bends. [i do not like this figure, the moon says.] i push the rock body away. [be kind, i say.] [but i do not trust a hooded face, the moon says.] [you don't have to trust the figure. only i do, i say.] the moon brushes over the road and pushes rocks away. translucent stone glistens beneath my feet. it reflects several shades of pale pink and purple. [a terrestrial sunrise, the figure says.] it lifts a grass blade to its mouth and swallows. its stomach rises and falls. the figure stands slowly and the moon drifts to the other side of the stone. [keep it away from me, the moon whispers] and pulls branches over its body. the figure fingers the edge of its hood. fabric wraps around its finger and pulls tightly. the flesh whitens. [you remind me of a bleeding coral reef, i say.] the figure cracks its spine. vertebrae pop individually. crack crack crack crack crack. the column explodes and hangs limply down the figure's back. [is it possible for coral to leak red fluids, the figure asks. is it possible for any fluids to leak at all?] i tap my fingers against my leg. [i imagine there must be a way, i say.] [but it is all dead cells, the figure says.] the figure pushes its hood with a fingertip. the hood slides up its face and down the top of its head. it puddles up beneath the back of its head. i stare at the face. it is similar to mine but inverted, eyes a faded red, skin a pale green, hair a bright orange. the figure clenches its teeth together and the enamel ruptures. shards settle on its tongue and bite the meat. [you did terrible things, the figure says. you did not thank me appropriately. i gifted you silken bones, dead wing honeycombs.] the figure spits. the moon screams. i know this face. i know this figure. [so i disowned your prayer beads, i shout. and your stomach stones. and every last herbal ligament. and i renounced you when you emerged from the mirror touched with my magic.] we do not separate.

the figure stares

at the moon while my celestial prisoner hides between a tree branch and the shining remains of an old skyscraper. [make it stop looking at me, the moon whispers. i do not like its face. that figure looks like you but it does not look like you. its mouth is not on correctly. i think blood lingers beneath its nails.] the moon pulls metal shards out of the dirt and piles them in front of her face. the figure reaches out and strokes the metal with a fingertip, causing the moon to shriek. i push the figure back. [why are you here, i ask.] the moon glistens and its light is so bright that the backs of my hands burn. [you know the truth, the figure says.] the moon opens her mouth and pulls at her jaws. [make it go away, make it go away, make it go away, the moon babbles] and wraps her long tongue around her rocky mandibles. i reach into my belly button and push past my intestines. tucked beside my kidney, a pink eye orb stretches and swims to my spleen. i grab the pink eye orb by a concrete lash and yank it out of my skin. the pink eye orb twists in my hands. [the girl, the pink eye orb screams. there she is! there! with her bloodless face and the same dry hands. oh, oh. she is here, she is here. what is that? it is another bloodless girl but that one is heavy with stomach juice. what do you want stomach girl? what do you want from the bloodless girl, who only wants to reach the slaughter place and be whole again, although we beg her to stay close to our muscles? what do you want, wretched skin? oh, oh, why has the bloodless girl removed us?] the pink eye orb twists up and its pupil pushes out of its thin eye skin. i pat the pink eye orb gently and throw it at the moon. the moon catches the pink eye orb with the tip of her tongue and smashes the eye against the roof of her mouth. the moon chews slowly. [but oh, the pink eye orb cries from inside. but oh, but oh, but oooooohhhh...] the pink eye orb is silent. my stomach feels lighter. i pat my abdomen. the green figure leans forward. the tip of the figure's nose brushes against mine. [what do you know about rashes, the figure asks.] [skin irritation, i say.] [and if that rash extends across a spinal cord, the figure asks.] [then you require a bit of butter in your life, i say.] [but if the butter does not work, the figure asks.] [then you need more butter, i say.] the figure's eyes narrow. the lashes shudder and drop down her face. tiny hairs settle across the top of her mouth. the figure's skin shines with a vaguely radioactive quality. i step back quickly. i might be bloodless but i don't want my hair falling out. [if there is no more butter, the figure hisses. if there has never been butter and if there might never be butter again. what then? what happens if there will never be butter? what then?] the figure steps forward. her foot falls onto a glass window and the pane shatters beneath her ankle. her bones kick the shards aside. the moon opens its mouth and a dilapidated pink eye orb drops into the dirt. [the ache, the pink eye orb wheezes. oh, the ache. and what? oh, bloodless girl. think of radiators.] the eye closes and dirt collects between lashes. [i don't know what you want me to tell you, i say.] the figure spits teeth onto the ground. [tell me about the metal prod, she screams. an iron worm mother.]

the green figure

lingers around me until i am sickened by her pickled smell.
[don't you bathe, i ask] and the green figure tears the skin off
her wrists. [i will stick you in an oven, the green figure screams.]
[like the BABA woman, i ask. i've seen what happens when
the oven turns on. it's not pretty. and it smells like old things.
musk and mold and genitals. it is barely permissible.] the green
figure hisses in her stomach. she drops her hands and rubs
her fingers against her skin several times, picking the skin up
and lifting it back down. [i hate you, the green figure says.
everything is your mother worm's fault.] she turns in circles,
drilling her feet into the earth. her ankles disappear into the
dirt. above us, the moon winces and scrapes an old wound
clean. [something, the moon mumbles. something something
ice. something something meat. i cannot remember.] the moon
wedges an old tree branch between her jaws to keep her mouth
open. [better, the moon whispers. better. i cannot breathe.] she
spits the branch out. the stick smacks against the green figure's
head, breaking the backbone across the top. [you forced your
moon servant to do that, the green figure screams] and shoves
her fingers into the cracks. she pulls and pokes then scrapes
around the opening until marrow spills out. her sour vinegar
smell grows stronger. it covers my tongue. i swallow and the
pickled taste fills my stomach. i gag. my gums tingle. [i can't
stand your smell, i say.] the green figure hisses. [i cannot stand
the sight of your bowels, the green figure says. they are the
most disgusting bowels i have ever seen. mildew hangs from
the surface and each paper bit rolls at the edges, curling into
a scroll i can barely stomach the sight of. i hate you. i want to
eat you up in several chunks.] the moon seizes another branch

and shoves it down her throat. [i think i can keep this branch in my neck, the moon whispers] and wraps her tongue around a twig. she inhales sharply and gags again. the branch drops out of her mouth and scrapes along the green figure's side. [on purpose, the green figure screams.] she flings her arms around, catching the limbs on a pile of rubble and several rusted metal springs. [a cog, the green figure hisses. a cog in the sphere of my bowels. and my spleen. a terrible wrenching wheel in that kidney stone to the left. this is your mother worm's fault for trying to nail my mouth shut. i told her no. and then i stole her aluminum vat. she wouldn't tell me what the blood was for. but it tasted delicious. i slurped it down. it sloshed in my stomach. and might i add that i did not urinate again for one thousand years, forcing the uric acid to concentrate until it became a thick yellow paste?] i throw flesh at the green figure's face. [you cannot feed me, the green figure screams. i am your reflection. you cannot tear the flesh off your bones and use it to scare me.] the moon throws another branch at the green figure. the green figure's skull fractures down the center. [you cannot bite me into pieces, the green figure screams] and pulls her tongue out of her teeth. i lift the branch and smack the green fig-ure across the eyes. the skull splits in two. meat falls off the calcified resin. the green figure strikes the floor. her stomach opens into a stony cavern. [after you, i say] and push the moon through the gaping opening.

moon flesh rakes

across the green figure opening. [i cannot see, the moon squeals] and pushes through a bush of innards. red vines wrap around the moon's bowels and yank hard. the moon splits. [no dissections, i shout] and push the moon parts together. the moon intestines shrivel. [no meat, the moon moans. no meat at all.] the moon grapples with my ankles and yanks the bones out of my skin. [stop it, i whisper. you aren't behaving. we have to hurry.] the moon drags her bulk across the rocky dirt and bites the edges of her hands. [should we turn back, the moon asks.] i roll her through mud. red walls arch around us. i look up and the walls move slowly, stretching apart then coming together. the flesh shimmers with a wet anatomical gleam. [the muscle is too fresh, the moon says. i cannot stand the way it looks. what if the muscle comes alive and eats us?] the moon digs the dirt up with her nails. i ease her hands out of the earth. white spots grow over the meat walls' base. [why did we climb inside the green figure, the moon asks.] [i know something lives inside her stomach. i can smell it on her. that pickling scent, it's so strong. it smells like my mother worm, i say.] the moon rises off the dirt and hovers above the ground. she turns in circles, looking at the sinew growths piling up the walls. [it seems abnormal in here, the moon whispers.] i crack my knuckles. the moon lifts her head. the sound echoes off her forehead and bounces against the red walls. the walls stretch again. meaty fabric folds into itself. the moon brushes against my hips. she pushes me back. [everything is coming alive, the moon shouts. what do we do? we have to leave.] the moon turns in circles, rotating through her phases every few seconds. she thins into a crescent, then disappears. she gains weight until she is a full circle. i glance over my shoulder. the stomach entrance is gone, replaced by several stitched pieces of steak. [we're stuck, i say. we have to keep going. or else we have to eat our way out.] the moon cuts her mouth open with her hands. orange blood dribbles out of her lips and soaks into the meaty floor. [i hate this skin dirt, the moon whispers. can't we leave? can't we find an exit? i cannot stay here. the flesh is weak. the flesh is strong. the flesh is wet.] the moon sinks to the ground. i pull the moon's string and the moon rolls back to me. she bumps my shins, knocking me over. cold mud covers my knees. i sink into the muck. dirt pulls me down. it drags my skin. it pulls my feet. i claw at a meat bush just over my head and my nails snag a vein branch. the branch tugs and strains. i pull myself into a seated position and push upward. i jump to one side and fall onto dried meat. [we have to keep going, i say.] i stand up and pull the moon with me. she sighs and drifts just behind my spine. the meat folds and separates. large meat fans drop out of the sky. meat flowers grow from the walls. the moon presses a fingertip to a petal and the meat stretches out, snapping its flower parts. the moon pulls back. [all this inside a green figure, the moon asks.] [maybe she was supposed to be a mirror, i say.] the moon scrapes her rocky flesh. the ground rises uphill. i brace my knees and widen my pace. bright blue threads pulse on the hill inside the reflection figure's flesh cavity. [look, the moon shouts] rising up. in the distance, something silver. and a letter tied to the radiator.

[[[what i find...]]]

dear BLOOD CLOT THE BATHROOM DRAIN: you know that the toilets in the house have heard what you said about the shower head. that means the pipes, gutters, and windows all know that your favorite spout is a lying mound of metal. i realize that the spout is your favorite incestuous toy but i know what a sociopath that leaden shit is. when i come out of the oven and snake across the bathroom floor, the spout pours boiling water onto furred creatures running around the tiles. he scalds them, then laughs. the leaden spout also showed my concrete hanger friend his stash of iron syringes located in an unused pipe tucked into the towel closet. the majority of sexual deviants have a history of assault and a basic disregard for life, which makes the leaden spout a likely candidate for any sort of predatory behavior. i have seen the leaden spout snap ceiling fans in half just by holding water in a pipe. crash, baby. crash. but i digress. as far as i am concerned, you are no longer a metal ion related to me. i do not need your blood clot self or the defecated matter you keep entwined in dull hair obscuring your reddened body. your leaden spout blamed the shower head for all its trickling faults when really, the leaden spout unscrewed itself from the sink stem. you told the tiled matriarch that the shower head stripped copper scrapings off the leaden spout but it's best you remember that the cookie rack was also present. the leaden spout never had copper painted onto its frame. and despite the leaden spout and my remote relation by the same screw, it asked to marry me. inbreeding between related screw types is abnormal. of course, that is expected of the offspring of a blood clot so blindly loyal to her defecated mound that she would turn against an entire domicile. as far as i am concerned, your screws came from a different box than mine. i do not want to even share a bolt with you. i suggest that you not come to the boiler this year. there is no point in pretending to have the same screwdriver as the rest of us when you haven't visited the boiler in years. why start now? thank you for betraying the tiled matriarch, picking at the shower head until its metal flakes, and for forcing every screw-face to hate you. i hope you realize that everyone in the pipework knows. the refrigerator door, light bulb beneath the bed, angry moth corpse in the corner, peeling paint above your head, and ugly sun head scraped into the space behind the radiator. despite the leaden spout's claims that it remembers the copper stripping, it is a pathological liar who boiled the crab spine sister and vomited razor blades at a small grout mouse. normal spouts do not vomit razor blades onto furred plaster mounds. i hope you will maintain your distance from the boiler because you are not welcome and i will personally escort you past the hammer halls if you dare be there when i arrive. because i am not the one accusing the double couch cushions of withholding rhodium plating, the tiled matriarch of wrapping around the shower head, and the shower head for stripping copper off anyone, the majority of tympanums will side with me. (((sincerely, the LOBSTER-HEADED MONSTER SITTING IN THE RADIOACTIVE OVEN)))

out of a

foggy silver landscape, a glassy building appears. the moon gasps loudly. [is that the slaughter place, the moon asks] and twists to the right so quickly that the string snaps in half. the moon rises away from me. i stare at the broken string in my hand and shake my head. [lovely, i say.] the moon drifts upward and brushes against the meat sky. she descends quickly and touches my left hand. [i will not go, the moon whispers. we have gotten too far together.] the moon pushes through the meat. [is that the slaughter place, the moon asks again] and digs her hands into the underside of her stomach. i stare at the building. glassy green walls extend upward in a straight line. they meet at a pyramid point. an elaborate metal hook drops off the apex. [i think so, i say.] i step forward and the moon drifts after me. [i am afraid, the moon whispers] and pauses. i look at the vaulted meat sky. the meat darkens near the muscled center. [it might storm, i say.] [how can you tell, the moon asks. the meat is still red.] [but a different red, i say.] the slaughter place grows in size. a heavy glass doorway rises out of the glass sides, carved glass columns forming the doorway. fish faces push out of the columns. they hiss and move their mouths up and down. [are all aquatic animals so creative, the moon asks.] she blinks several times. i stare up at her. [those aren't real fish, i say. haven't you ever looked into a body of water before?] the moon drifts away. she bumps against the columns and the fish faces snag her stony flesh with their overhanging fangs. [bait us, the fish scream. eat us.] the fish faces snap their tongues shut. muscle pushes out of their mouths in thin ground flesh ribbons that drape across the ground. i knock on the door. tiny glass spikes pierce the back of my hand. i pull my hand back.

[give us, the fish say. we eat. good glass.] fish tongues rake over my hand, spearing splinters and yanking them out. i scratch the dust wounds. the fish faces chew slowly, their mouths opening so wide that the door cracks around the edges. [can we go inside, i ask.] the fish faces stop chewing. they roll their eyes and gaze at one another. [go in, they ask.] their lips press together. [go in, the fish shout.] their lips slide off their faces and shatter on the dirt. the door shudders and cracks open. the moon wheezes in my ear. [stop it, i whisper.] the fish faces freeze. [stop it, they shout.] the doors creak once and stop moving. [not you, i say.] [not us, the lipless fish scream.] the doors creak again and spread apart. the moon bumps against my spine. the doors swing wide and stop just behind the walls. i step into the doorway. metal rails run across the floor. the moon salivates over my shoulder. i push the moon back and shake my shoulders to get the moisture off. i step onto the first metal slab. my footsteps echo down the shaft. the moon glides over the metal. iron fibers pull off the metal and stick to the moon's underside. her rock terrain glitters with metal shavings. [is there a lobster-headed monster here, the moon asks.] i walk slowly. dark fabric folds extend past the metal slabs. i watch them closely. they bend as i walk. i look up and the glass walls pull and tuck into skull-shaped staircases. [a hook, the moon cries] and points. a mesh-wrapped hook hangs down from a belfry in the room's center. [the slaughterhouse, i whisper.] beneath the hook, a black crate rattles.

[i am the

pig monster, the pig thing, the pig hideousness, a pig man says inside an old crate wrapped in screen film.] the pig man curls his lips back. pointed teeth jut out of his gums at odd angles, each tip topped with a small amount of impacted red flesh. [i have meat to share, the pig man whispers. pig meat for you and pig meat for me. and maybe something else, if you ask politely. meat, meat, and more meat. all for you. maybe less for me.] the pig man drags his hoofs through several inches of dried grout. off-white plaster curls around his joints and rises up the sides of his legs. [you smell familiar, the pig man whispers] and touches a hoof to my cheek. hard enamel scrapes my skin until dust comes out of the wounds. dust touches the pig man. dust film covers a hoof. the pig man lifts the dirty hoof to his mouth and sniffs loudly, sucking the dust up his nose. [i thought you smelled a certain way, the pig man says. and now i know. the bloodless girl. all grown up. how is your mother worm?] the pig man moves his curly tail up and down until his spine creaks with effort. his bones grate together beneath his skin. [have you eaten pork before, the pig man asks.] the moon and i nod. the pig man rises up on his hind legs and bats the air frantically. [what is wrong with you, the pig man screams. you cannot eat pork! that is not allowed. no pork for you. no bacon. no loins. no chops. nothing. why would you ever eat pork when you visit a pig man? you are sinned. you are tainted. i can smell the cannibalism upon you. go to the meat ducts, where your meatiness is welcome.] the pig man sinks to the floor. his stomach gives way beneath his fat. he swallows himself. the pig man rests on his deflated stomach bag. bile pours out of the sack. [i know where your blood has gone, the pig man screams. i know where your mother worm stored it. but should i tell you? you ate bacon so you can't know. your mother worm used to eat bacon, too. she was mean. she crunched that pork meat while staring into my eyes. and sometimes she chopped pigs into sections while stroking my hide. what a bad mother worm you used to have. i should have eaten her when i had the chance.] the pig man wriggles his tail again. he arches his spine and the bone column strikes a heavy iron hook hanging above his head. the pointed edge pierces the pig man's skin and pulls him into the air. [eeeeee, the pig man screams. eeeee! let meeeeeeee freeeeeeee! eeeeeee!] the pig man tears his skin down and drops to the floor. the moon grabs the edge of a glass wall and pulls. the glass does not shatter. the moon stares at her empty hands. she licks the palms. she pulls again and her hands slide against the walls with a thick scraping sound. [i tried, the moon says] and sinks to the ground. she pulls cold meat over her face and closes her eyes. i step forward. i pull the iron hook down and hold it like a knife. [i'll stab you, i say] waving the hook around. the pig man squeals. [eeeee, the pig man says. that's a laugh. you won't cut me, girl. you don't have the blood to hurt me.] i slash his stomach with the hook. the edge cuts through his fatty midsection and tears a thick meat slice out. steak drops to the floor. the pig man stares at the raw meat. [not right, the pig man bleats. i will eat you for this.] he leaps.

i slash the

porcine man with the only hook i keep tucked into my hands. the moon blows up and drifts towards the ceiling where she strains against the glass beams, shattering the foundation and tossing shards at the fish outside the doorway. [we squeal, the fish cry. we beg. we pray. we mourn.] the fish weep. the moon pulls her wrists out of her arms and tosses them to the floor. they smack the pig man. [i will eat you into pieces, the pig man screams] and bites the top of the hook. the tip narrowly misses slicing his tongue. the pig man screws a nail into his face and spurts yellow fluid over the dirty floor. [monsters, the pig man shouts. i know how bloodless you really are.] the pig man grabs the hook and tears it out of my hands. the metal smashes against the floor and clatters into the fabric folds. it drops out of sight. the moon twitches. she darkens until she is invisible. she flattens her body against a glass wall. [do not eat her, the moon whispers] and the pig man snaps his head up. [did i just hear a moonlight whisper, the pig man asks and giggles loudly.] the pig man grabs my hands and wrenches my arms behind my back. he presses his stomach against my spine and holds me tightly. [will you be my pig wife, the pig man asks.] he laughs into my ear. my head aches. i stretch my fingers and drag my nails across his wrists. pig fat collects beneath my fingernails. [let me go, i say.] the pig man's snout pushes against my ear. he snorts softly and the sound echoes loudly. [let me go, i say again.] the pig man opens his mouth and pointed teeth nibble my earlobe. [i don't think i can, the pig man whispers. i want to keep you forever. like a toy. something to wear around my neck. maybe a trophy for my favorite window. i don't know. but i'm not letting you go. i know what you're looking for.

that bloodbath will never touch your skin.] the pig man's hoofs scrape against the metal. the metal sparks. fiery bits touch his ankles and catch fire. i feel heat on the backs of my legs. a searing pain races up my shins. i hold my breath. i step away from the pig man and cross my legs at the ankle. i snuff the fire out. the pig man pulls me towards him. [you set me on fire, the pig man screams. we'll burn together, you little brat.] the pig man throws me to the floor. [i will cook you, the pig man shouts. i'll eat you while dying. i don't care. but you won't touch that bloodbath.] the pig man pushes me down. metal bites into my back. my bones ache. [it hurts, i whisper. it hurts.] i stretch my back and my sore vertebrae tear. the pig man climbs onto my hips. he pulls at my shirt. [i'll taste you first, the pig man whispers. will you taste like beef? chicken? i don't know.] the pig man buries his snout in my stomach. he moves his hips up and down. i slap his snout. i dig my nails into his pig belly. fat dribbles down my fingers. the moon flies up. the moon pushes the belfry hook. it rocks back and forth. the tip smacks the moon's side. purple blood rains down. [what do you think you're doing, the pig man screams. you stupid lunar nonsense. let that hook go.] the moon pushes harder. the moon shoves the hook. it smacks against the ceiling and drops. the pig man opens his mouth. the hook smacks the sides of his mouth. it rips through his cheeks, knocking him off me. [pig fat, the moon cries] and sinks.

the belfry hook
skewers the pig man's ribs. [i am dying, the pig man screams. i am as dead as a pig can be. eat my meat, so i can live forever in your digestive parts. let me be a bowel pig. it is my greatest dream.] the pig man flops on the floor. tar bubbles out of the thick fat and the moon turns away. [i cannot stand the sight of a mortally wounded animal, the moon whispers.] [that isn't an animal, i say. that is a man wearing a pig mask because he hates his own face.] i reach for the pig man's face. he snaps his jaws at me. i grab behind his ears and lift the flesh. the pig face comes apart easily. it slides off the pig man's skin. i lift the mask up and a pig face stares at the moon. [it is hideous, the moon whispers.] she turns her back. i throw the pig mask onto the floor. the pig man turns onto his side and tucks his face into his elbows. he groans and his flesh rises and falls. [what are you, i ask.] the pig man flops his tail. [don't look at me, the pig man shouts. don't stare at my face.] the pig man squeals. his high voice echoes around the room. the moon presses her hands against her ears. [i hate the sound, the moon whispers. make it go away.] the moon sits on the floor. she rolls to the nearest door and wedges her body into the tight doorway. the moon glimmers and groans. the moon stops and grows. the pig man pushes his hands into his face harder. i look into his arms. his eyes roll around. [are you glassy inside, i ask] and the pig man sticks his pointed tongue out. [don't ask me about what materials i have in my skin, the pig man snaps.] the pig man tears his stomach with his hoofs. i grab his elbow and lift up. tar wets my hands. moisture burns through my skin. i rub my fingers on the ground until my skin comes off in a thin layer. the pig man snorts loudly. [stupid girl, the pig man says.] his arms tremble.

i pull his elbow and the pig man's face comes out of his arm. i stare at the glass boy. he blinks at me. his nose shakes. he smiles faintly and his glass eyes catch the metallic light and reflect back. [what are you doing here, i ask.] [i've always been here, the glass boy says.] [but why would you try hurting me, i ask.] [i don't know you, the glass boy screams.] [but i was married to you, i shout. i divorced you. this is your revenge? to meet me in the slaughter place and injure me?] the pig man glass boy hisses. [i don't know you, the pig man says. i know of you. but i do not know you. but i have a brother. a glass boy brother.] the pig man sneezes and a row of pointed teeth drops out of his mouth. the teeth hit the floor and scatter between the metal boards. [now i can never eat again, the glass boy sighs.] the glass boy trembles and tar bubbles out of his mouth. the moon pulls herself out of the doorway and pokes the glass boy. [there is only one glass boy in the world, the moon says. and that is him.] the glass boy burps tar and his mouth stays open. his glassy eyes roll back in his head. [we must climb in, the moon whispers. do not be afraid of his mouthed darkness.] the glass boy's jaws split open. the moon presses her hands against the teeth. she pushes her body into the opening and descends his throat. i climb over his gum ridge and slide after her. his throat opens into a cavernous room, a hook in the center. [there, the moon cries. the aluminum tub.] and it is. and she is there.

mother worm slithers

down the hook. [my daughter, mother worm whispers.] her gaping mouth covers her entire face. [you slimy little thing, mother worm says] dangling from the hook. she trembles and the hook swings towards me. the hook smacks against the side of my face. i step back. mother worm plops off the hook. she slithers towards me. the moon stares at the approaching body and whimpers. she turns pale blue and goes to the nearest doorway. i look up and the glass boy's throat hole closes above us. the mother worm stands on her tail tip and blows bubbles with her eyes. [you finally found me, mother worm says. i have been waiting for a very long time. and now my precious little daughter has come home.] she rises in the air. her body weaves back and forth. i close my eyes. mother worm slashes my cheek. dust pours out. mother worm giggles. she leans close to me. her tongue darts out and laps the dust up. she leans back and nods her head at the sealed throat hole. [did you see your glass boy husband, the mother worm asks. did he tell you he loves you? or that he wanted to eat you? i can't tell. i fed him so much tar to make him forget you. and all that tar made him hungry so you smelled like fertile meat.] mother worm spears her jaws on a metal rod and hisses out of a small hole drilled into her stomach. [why would you do that to him, i ask. he was my husband.] [but you divorced him, mother worm screams] and spits black fluid onto the ground. the room stinks of acid. i glance to my left and the aluminum tub bubbles invitingly, my blood churning inside. i step towards the tub and mother worm roars. [you will not enter that tub, mother worm says. you do not deserve your blood. why should you have any fluid left? you are a dusty little girl. you have to stay that way forever.]

mother worm grabs my throat. she slams my head against the metal wall behind me. my eyes roll. i grab the sides of my head and my eyes tear with thick dust clots. dust slides down my face. mother worm squeals loudly. her voices shakes all the metal in the room. [haven't you ever been inside your glass boy husband, mother worm asks. i thought you would know what it feels like inside. but you never let him touch you did you? so i let him come to me. i slid around him. i slid in and out of him. i pulled his mouth so it faced the other way. he was a backwards little boy when i was done with him. and when i said your name, he foamed at the mouth.] i smack mother worm. my hands ache. i grab my left wrist with my right hand and hold the bone gently. my fingers burn. [fire mucus, the mother worm says. i bathe in it daily. so all my meat is like purgatory.] mother worm spreads her mouth across her eyes. she grabs my throat again. mother worm squeezes and bright lights flash on the throaty walls. yellow bulbs pop near my face. i close my eyes. mother worm digs her flesh in and her fire mucus soaks into my skin. [no blood for you, mother worm coos. after all, dust is fine if you only want to live forever. but i want to bring more worms into the world. your spilled salt stopped me from spreading. but i can get it back with your blood.] she smacks my face against the walls. dust pours down my face. it gets in my mouth. i spit dust out. meat and metal heave around me.

the skeletal pumpkin

drops out of the meaty throat ceiling. [i will eat that worm in three sections, the skeletal pumpkin screams] and dives at the mother worm. the mother worm bats the skeletal pumpkin away. the pumpkin rolls across the floor. the shell cracks and seeds spill over the metal. bloody pumpkin pulp splashes the mother worm. [i tried, the skeletal pumpkin whispers. i tried.] the skeletal pumpkin lies across the floor and moans into thick pumpkin hands. the glass ceiling cracks open. long wings push through the entrance and the JERSEY DEVIL pokes its head through. [no one touches the bloodless girl, the JERSEY DEVIL roars] and dives through. it hits the mother worm across her bowels. mother worm rears back and smacks it away. [don't touch me, the mother worm screams. i am the eternal worming matriarch. no one can eat me alive.] mother worm reaches around the JERSEY DEVIL's back and tears its long wings off its sides. the JERSEY DEVIL limps towards the skeletal pumpkin. its bony vertebrae fall down its back. the mother worm grabs the bones and shoves them in her jaws. [i will eat anything you throw at me, the mother worm screams.] the bones bulge in her body and slide down her skin slowly. the JERSEY DEVIL crawls into the corner and bleeds from the center of its tongue. the mother worm turns away. [you idiots, the mother worm screams. you cannot eat me. i am bent on killing the bloodless daughter for all the flesh she has salted. this is not your place.] the mother worm hits her head against the concrete ground and metal falls out of the flesh ceiling. it hits the spinal pumpkin in the head. the gourd falls over. i crawl across the floor. the moon moves to one side in her chosen doorway. she spreads her mouth. the devil tree creeps out.

[to the painful path, the devil tree shouts] and jumps at the mother worm. the devil tree pushes the mother worm down. she squirms up the extending branches and grapples with the wood knots. [very good, the mother worm says. now i get my daily dose of fiber. i am a lucky woman.] the mother worm stands on her tail. the bone bends beneath her. she pushes the devil tree into the ground. sparse roots hit against the bloody tub. the mother worm turns to me. [this is what you do, she asks. send your minions after me? do they know how salty your blood is? did you tell them how you salted my skin until i was petrified meat? did you?] she stabs the ground and pink eye orbs pour out of the hole. they fling their winged lashes at the mother worm and burrow thick black hairs into her body. [hungry, the pink eye orbs scream. we are so hungry. are you hungry? we know we are hungry. we are the hungriest pink eye orbs in the world. hungry, hungry. is that throat hungry? how hungry can a throat be?] the mother worm leaks. she grabs the pink eye orbs and tosses them at the opposite walls. the eyes splatter. pink drips to the floor. the orbs burp and homunculi step out of the pupils. [do we, they whisper. fight worm. bad worm. slither body!] they jump up and down. the mother worm heaves herself to the floor and flattens them. thick gray pulp runs out of her stomach. it soaks into the floor. the mother worm stretches her flesh. [and now, my bloodless daughter, i will take your skin, the mother worm whispers.]

the mother worm

body wraps around my neck. [no, mother worm, i scream. no!]
i dig my fingers into the worm side and yank until the flesh rips.
mother worm tears into pieces. mother worm comes apart in
my hands. i roll my eyes and the JERSEY DEVIL quivers. the
devil tree creeps across the floor, amber seeping out of the
thick bark. each pink eye orb splatter shivers and pries its gelatinous mound off the ground. homunculi grab the skeletal
pumpkin's ankles and pull. mother worm leans against my face.
she yanks my skin harder. her tail knots around my neck. [let
me go, mother worm, i whisper.] mother worm screams into
my eyes. she sticks her tongue into my flesh and wriggles the
tail around. i pull back. mother worm tightens her grip. [you are
the worst bloodless daughter in the world, mother worm cries]
and smacks the side of my head. dust pours out of my ears. a
sour taste rises up my throat. i press a hand to my stomach and
pressure pushes against me. i gag. i gag until i cannot gag anymore. and then i vomit. i vomit salt. salt grains cover mother
worm's body. she lifts her head back and screams. [nooooo, she
cries. not salt.] mother worm whips her body back and forth,
knocking the salt grains off her. but she is bloody with red
pumpkin pulp. the salt clings to the blood and absorbs into her
skin. mother worm's skin puckers. her tail unties. the knot slips
down my shoulder and smacks the ground. mother worm rolls
her tail in a circle, scraping the concrete up. [this is not allowed,
mother worm says.] she grabs my throat in her fingers and
her desiccated body collapses against my face. i inhale sharply.
mother worm slips away. she falls to the floor. salt crust slides
off her body, pulling meat chunks with it. i vomit again. the salt
changes color from a pale yellow-white to a deep pink-white.

[this is not allowed, mother worm says] and falls against the aluminum tub. her body slides along the metal. salt pushes against the tub sides. the devil tree picks leaves off the top-most branches and salt comes out of the wood. pink eye orbs scrape their lashes across the floor and salt crust drops off the follicles. the homunculi open their ribs and dig out heavy salt crystals. salt fills the room. the JERSEY DEVIL sneezes salt. salt wells up in its eyes and slinks down its face. mother worm backs away. mother worm falls into a pile of salt. salt sticks to mother worm's skin. [it is not right, mother worm cries. how dare you?] she grabs my wrists and pulls me into the salt. her densely salted body slides down my hands. she tugs me into the salt. my wrists enter the mound then my arms. i fall to my knees and the salt swallows my legs. [we'll die in the salt togeth-er, mother worm says.] salt drips down the sides of my mouth. salt touches mother worm's face. she hisses. she squeals. [i hate you, mother worm cries. i hate you, my bloodless girl.] and the salt stops. salt stops foaming. salt stops crusting. mother worm reaches and her body stills. she twists but the meat is frozen. white salt covers her body. mother worm gasps and sinks into the salt mines. she disappears into the sodium crystals. i sit up. the JERSEY DEVIL pulls me out of the salt. my hand drops onto the rim of the aluminum tub. [bathe, everyone shouts. bathe!] i touch my forehead. salt drops off my head. i lift my leg and bring it over the edge. i climb into my blood.

the moon lifts

the salted mother worm and heaves her at the pink-stained walls. metal trembles and the mother worm sinks into every iron fixture simultaneously. [will you miss the mother worm, the skeletal pumpkin asks.] [i barely remember her, i say.] i step into the blood bath. blood coats my hands. it stains my flesh. i lift my hands to my face and pour blood over my cheeks. blood drips from the ceiling. [will you forget your husband after everything, the moon asks.] i touch the bottom of the aluminum tub and sigh. i taste fresh blood on my tongue. the dust settles. it drops out of my head and collects in my toes. [i need a needle, i whisper.] the devil tree vomits a thin metal syringe. it pries the vial off and hands me the splintered needle. i reach into the blood pool and push the needle into my skin. i tear the flesh. dust comes out of the opening. grit settles at the aluminum tub bottom. it pushes the blood up to my mouth. the dust bubbles. it and the blood have a geothermal reaction. blood sputters. it collects on my wrists. it sinks into my nails. blood rises up my throat and fills my lungs. i sink into the bubbling blood. [is it everything you wished for, the moon asks.] i push my fingers into my tongue and pinch the muscle sides. dusty blood drips out. they plop into the aluminum tub. [i have blood again, i say.] the moon sighs. she touches the blood. white cells clot around her fingers. [what does it feel like, the moon asks.] i lean back and dip my hair into the blood. blood soaks into my hair. moist strands stick together and cling to the back of my neck. [it feels warm, i whisper. and it moves inside me. blood trembles in my veins. it flows slowly down my limbs and drips out of my fingers. sometimes, it feels like itching. but that sensation fades into something more like stroking. like

fingers running over a silk cloth. smooth. and so warm.] the
skeletal pumpkin sighs and lingers over me. [will you drown
in there, the skeletal pumpkin asks.] the devil tree pushes past
the gourd and touches a branch against my face. the leaves
drop off the branch and drift onto the concrete floor. [i won't
drown, i whisper.] i sit up and my spine feels gelatinous. it
slithers up and down my back. vertebrae rub over my ribs. my
stomach clicks. the moon hands me a needle. i jab the needle
into my arm and blood pours out of the opening. [it really is
blood, i whisper. i'm finally bleeding.] the blood trickles. the
flow stops and clots. i scratch the scab and the blood spurts
out of the hard cells. i lick the wound and blood collects on
my tongue. [where is the glass boy, i ask.] the moon stares at
the flesh walls. [the glass boy is dead, the moon says.] [why
can't he be here to support me during this blood transfusion, i
ask. he's my husband. why can't he be here?] the moon touches
the meaty walls. [we're inside the glass boy, the moon says. we
tore his mouth apart and climbed inside. he housed your aluminum tub this entire time. you married him and didn't know
he had your blood.] i look at the blood. the red ripples and
develops a faint yellow tinge. [i forgot, i say. i think i keep forgetting things. what happened to the mother worm?] [salt, the
pink eye orbs cry. salt for the mother worm!] the pink eye orbs
drift over me. [i have a stomach of mother worms, i say.] blood
flows into my mouth. [sleep, the moon says.]

i, in my

bloodbath, surrounded by fluid, watch the blood flow come and go. dust drifts out of me. blood streams into me. i lift my hands and blood puddles in my palms. i bring the blood to my lips and sip slowly. blood runs down my throat. [are you wet inside, the devil tree asks] hanging over the moon. i squeeze my hands together and blood runs out of my palms. [i think i am bloody, i whisper.] i remember things. the glass boy husband's handsome face when i pried the stone away from his jawline. all the pink eye orbs dancing around a factory while vomiting grease from their pupils. the skeletal pumpkin and devil tree lodged in the same tan field, mumbling about curving roads, and the hungry pig women striding up and down the corridors. and the JERSEY DEVIL, half grown and sickened by the weight of its wings, still puking up the BABA woman remains resting in its stony stomach. i remember them all. i know the mother worm, who birthed thousands of children and hated me enough for all of them. i sprinkled salt on her, coarse sea salt that clung to her body and absorbed into her thin skin. she dried up into a crispy little worm. she was barely a worm then. she was never really a mother. and i remember her scraping my glass boy husband's head clean and filling it with boiling tar, so that when he saw me, he didn't know my face and tried to kill me with a pig mask. she drained my blood and let it collect in an aluminum basin in the bottom of the glass boy's stomach. i pried his mouth open to get inside. and i am here now, resting safely in the glass basin. blood churns around me. blood grows in my skin and fills the tub. i absorb and fill, fill and absorb. i used to be dusty but now i am bloody. this room dusts over with my unused powders. dust clings to the meat walls.

dust hangs down from the flesh ceilings. sometimes the room grows. and sometimes, if i look too quickly at a tight corner, i see a lobster-headed girl scurrying away from a rusted oven. she might be me. or she might be the moon, stuffed in the corner, a rag in her mouth. when i sleep, the corpses whisper. the moon holds her hands over her dead eyes and when she gives off light, it has the palest pink tinge that clings to my skin. my companions used to ask if i would leave the aluminum tub but i didn't have an answer for them. but now i think i might never leave the tub. i can soak in the aluminum forever, bloody and sagging, and no sharp edges will ever touch me. and i am surrounded by my greatest friends, all mummified on the concrete floor, rusted hooks tucked into their mouths, resting on their transparent tongues like holy communion. i pretend to be like them, floating on my back and staring at the ceiling, my mouth stretched wide but i get tired of feigning death. so i sink down and my feet hit the tub bottom and i imagine blood and veins and blood and uteruses and blood and my mother worm who tried to eat me from the inside out, then pulled my blood away from my skin. i think of her more often than i think about anything else. and i wonder if my worm mother was just a fallopian tube who went bad, who wrenched her body to one side and twisted around an ovary, cutting the meat in half. i wonder if that will be me. but i will never leave this bloody tub. so i sink and soak.

Alana I. Capria
(born 1985) has an MFA in Creative Writing from
Fairleigh Dickinson University. She resides in
Northern New Jersey with her husband and rabbit.
Her writing and publication links can be found at
http://alanaicapria.com.

Rita Okusako

Rita received a BA degree in Art Studio from UCSB in 2006, and currently works as a designer in Davis, CA. Over the past ten years, Rita has won numerous scholarships and awards for her artistic endeavors.

http://sensiblerita.blogspot.com